ELEVEN

A Short Story Collection

A V IAIN

Contents

SUBMARINE

YVONNE SLAMMED THE DOOR SHUT. Adrenalin seized her muscles as she twisted the wheel to secure the lock. Fists pounded against the other side, but nonetheless she felt safe—back in her examination room.

Her blood dribbled onto the floor, already making a puddle about her feet. She rushed across the room to the cabinet and withdrew the iodine, some cotton wool and a roll of gauze. No anaesthetic, she needed her wits about her.

Hands shaking, Yvonne unscrewed the iodine bottle. She paused and took a couple of deep breaths. She needed to relax. There was no way he could get in.

She inspected her arm. The gaping wound oozed crimson. With her good hand, she tipped iodine onto the cotton wool then pressed it on her arm.

Contorted breathing and scraping came from the other side of the door.

After running the tap and splashing water on the cut, she put more cotton wool on the wound, but the blood seeped through in a matter of seconds. Desperate, she piled on more and more until she needed a gauze to keep it in place.

She staggered across the room, the adrenaline from the chase eking from her system and making her feel faint. She fumbled through the drawer, sending instruments clattering to the ground. Finally she located the scissors. She leant against the wall as she went about strapping up her arm.

She considered why she was so anxious to stay alive. What was keeping her going? They must've hit the outer limit of cruising depth, somewhere around eight-hundred feet below the surface of the sea, and the damaged engines kept rolling on without enough power to get back up.

She braced her hands on her knees. The scraping got louder. Sweat dampened her spine. Should she let the maniac in? Let him put an end to her misery?

Already blood came through the gauze. She grabbed her surgical sutures from the shelf then she sat down on the bed. Her hands trembled as she threaded the needle. She looked at her bandaged arm, thinking of what she was about to do.

She took a deep breath and ripped the gauze from her arm. It stung and she had to bite her tongue to stop herself screaming.

After placing the browned gauze on the bed, she collected up the bottle of iodine and squeezed more onto her cut. Inside she screeched. Her toes curled in pain. She applied more pressure. The blood retreated and she readied the needle and thread.

The first prick made her flinch. She watched the black bead of blood emerge on her white skin. She tried to pep herself up for the next stab. Teeth clenched, she stuck the needle in deep and hard.

She gasped, but went on—forcing the needle through and bringing it out the other side, making a neat loop in the thread. She repeated the action. Her face reddened, but her medical brain took over—reducing the situation to theory, a series of diagrams.

In twenty-one stitches it was all over. She tied off the last one and collapsed against the padded wall. Her heart pounded. She concentrated on keeping herself conscious. Passing out could be fatal—blood would seep out while she slept.

Above her, the light flickered.

They were down deep. She wondered if the electrics could take the pressure. Probably. One thing she'd learnt from life aboard submarines was that machines outlived humans.

Drip . . . Drip . . .

The sound came from the hall. Perhaps a pipe had burst. It got louder—the sound of footsteps. "Yvonne?"

The voice sent chills through her body. She didn't answer.

"Yvonne?" Metal tapped the door.

The knife. Yvonne squeezed her eyes shut and tried not to imagine the face—full of creases and pockmarks.

"Open the door, Yvonne."

Tears formed in her eyes and she bit her lip to stop herself crying. "No," she said.

"Yvonne."

"NO!" She bolted across the room and smashed her good fist against the door.

The sound of footsteps scurried back down the corridor.

Yvonne put her head in her hands and sobbed. What was she going to do? She looked around the room. Would she ever see anything outside this room's familiar nooks and crannies—its cold bed which had taken every man's backside while she'd examined them—the same bed where she had conceived the baby and lost it soon after?

Her gaze settled on the instruments on her side table. The syringes, blades and pills laid out—solutions to all her problems. She had thought about them over the past weeks, ever since the captain had told her he was discharging her at the next port.

The dripping got louder.

She pulled her hands away from her face and went across the room. The bottle of pills fit neatly in her hand. Inside, she inspected the bright yellow capsules. She shook the bottle, letting them collide against each other. It would take about thirty to put her out of service.

She unscrewed the lid and scattered them into her palm: Little yellow fire exits.

The door squeaked.

Her head jerked around and the pills spilled onto the floor.

The door sprang open.

Yvonne's breath hitched in her throat. How had he got the

door open? Pills forgotten, she grabbed a scalpel then crept toward the door. She stared out into the corridor.

Hanging from the roof by a rope was Carlson—the lieutenant—his stomach slit open and guts hanging out.

Bile soured her tongue and she dropped the scalpel. The maniac had sliced Carlson from his ribcage to his belly button then strung him up for her to see.

Her eyes darted about the corridor, trying to make out the maniac. He must have been nearby watching her reaction—enjoying seeing her squirm. She inched out into the corridor.

She edged round the body, her eyes widening in morbid fascination—taking in each gory detail of the maniac's work. The initial wound ran up Carlson's front, down to the last brutal stroke. The organs hung out, dripping blood into an ever-growing, red-brown pool at his feet. A glint of light caught her eye. Yvonne bent down.

At Carlson's feet lay the bloodied knife.

Shivering, she got to her feet and walked on into the submarine's belly.

The first junction presented her with the option of going up to the sailors' quarters—where this had all started—or down to the cargo deck. However, she ignored both, continuing onward—to the captain's quarters. She needed to find out what had happened. As far as she knew, the captain was the only other one left alive.

Her eye sockets ached as she tried to peel back the gloom. She stayed alert to any sound. Behind her, the dripping faded as she proceeded along the corridor.

She hazarded a look back at Carlson's body. It reminded her of the pigs hanging off meat hooks she'd seen at the market when she was little.

She reached the captain's cabin without seeing the maniac.

She rapped on the door. A low murmur came from inside and she turned the wheel. It wasn't locked.

Portraits peered down on her as she entered. To one side the captain's boots sat, as if worn by a phantom guard. She turned back and locked the door.

The captain sat on the floor with his back against the bunk—his face contorted in pain. He turned to her. "Wha . . ." He drew a gasping breath. "What do you want?"

She stepped closer.

He winced.

She paused, considering whether her presence made him uncomfortable. She knew captains were proud men, unlikely to want to share their private dying moments—moments of weakness—with those of inferior rank. Nonetheless, she continued to help him—aware her medical skills could help prolong his life or —at least—put an end to his suffering. She crouched alongside.

He turned to the wall. "Go away."

When she inspected his body, she noticed his tracksuit trousers were stained with blood. "Let me help. Do you have some scissors?"

The captain didn't reply.

She rose and went over to the large writing desk, where she supposed the scissors were kept. Some of the drawers already stood open, so she went through those first.

The captain groaned.

She spun round, thinking the maniac had come back to finish him off. However, there was nothing but her reflection—looking back from the mirror. The captain lay in the same place.

The scissors were in the second drawer down. Although they weren't ideal—designed for paper—she couldn't risk crossing the corridor again. She returned to the captain's side and went to work on the trouser leg.

Arms outstretched, the captain lunged at her. "You bitch!"

She backed up, the scissors clutched to her chest. She was used to aggression from her patients—enlisted men—but it was strange to hear anger from those of rank. She recognised the hatred in the captain's eyes. "What's wrong?"

"What's wrong?" The captain sneered. "You *bitch*."

Their eyes remained fixed together for a few more moments then the captain broke it off.

She went back to cutting material. Soon, she reached the knee. The cut was terrible. Much deeper than the one the maniac had inflicted on her. "Do you have any iodine?"

The captain didn't reply.

Across the room, she eyed a portrait of the captain with his family. The captain stood up straight dressed in his uniform. His wife, about half a foot shorter, stood to his right. Their son— perhaps three or four years old—sat on a chair in front, dressed in a blue sailor's suit. Something about the photograph struck her as Victorian. The way they were organised.

She looked from the captain's knees to his white face. He didn't look neat or composed now.

The captain shook his head. His eyes were wet with tears. "Why did you do it?"

She felt numb, as if she'd plunged into an ice bath headfirst. "What?"

"I thought you were going to keep it together. Don't you remember our agreement?"

She shook her head. Confusion descended over her like a cloud of steam.

The captain continued, "Why? What purpose did it serve?"

Suddenly, the memories came back—like a high-definition television image. The captain's weight on her. His sweaty skin. His pants and groans. The damp feeling inside her afterward. The family she'd never have. The screams as—one-by-one—

she'd killed the crew. A headache gripped her brain, shutting everything else off.

The captain clenched his eyes tight, like a dog anticipating a smack from its owner.

She snatched up the portrait and plunged the corner of the frame into the captain's damaged leg. The frail glass shattered and entered his butter-skin.

Screams filled the air, pushing her on. She swiped the portrait across the captain's throat, slicing through his trachea and vocal chords. The screaming stopped and he made a hissing sound.

Standing over him, she watched the life creep from his body. He reached up to her, but she batted his arm away—like a kitten knocking away a ball of string.

Then she saw the safety valves, housed behind glass—to one side of the captain's bunk. She approached them. After a moment's hesitation, she reached out to turn the bright yellow handle.

Inside there were three valves: Oxygen, Main Tank and Reserves. She turned them all to zero then sat back on the captain's bunk with the broken portrait of the captain's family staring back up at her from the floor.

THE MAN IN THE MURDERER

1

OH, I SAW IT ALL, of that there's no doubt. What I might be nudged into telling you, though, is another matter altogether.

It was a fierce, icy night on the street where I live, Dorchester Avenue for those interested. And I recall quite clearly standing at my window, as I do quite often, looking out through my netted curtains into the street. I suppose if you were around here, talked to a few of the neighbours you'd get a good idea that I have something of a reputation as what you might call a—*ahem*—curtain twitcher.

I remember pressing my forehead up against the glass and looking out. As is usual, I started looking from the top of the street—the house in which the Savages live—before working my way down, to the Norwiches, after them the Selferns, the Pearces, Fordes, Lunnocks, and so on, right the way around to where my line of sight ends.

The Partridges.

The Partridges, it has to be said, have the nicest house on the street. Although we all do our best to keep up appearances, to keep our windows clean of dust, our driveways clear of leaves and our doorknobs brightly polished, the Partridges just manage to keep their home . . . well let's say just a little more than spotless.

They always struck me as a *respectable* family, the Partridges, the way that they had those two blond children—one boy and one girl—and the way they would make their way along the street in their winter coats, all of them with a scarf tucked into their collars, and—without exception—each wearing a flawless smile. Once, I remember the mother—Anne, if I recall correctly —yes, I remember the steady *clack* of her heels coming up the

13

concrete steps to my front door, and that efficient pair of knocks on my brass knocker.

That was the first time I saw her up close. Now, I'd be first to admit—in my life as a bachelor—that I'm most likely more susceptible to feminine beauty than most, but she blew in through my doorway like, uh . . . like a warm summer breeze, if you'll excuse the trite turn of phrase.

That steady scent of peaches reminded me of my father's farm, back when I was a boy—we kept a fairly extensive orchard, you see. And then I took in the gloss sticking to her lips. She reminded me a bit, in that moment, of the car they keep in the driveway—the one that I would see Adam Partridge waxing within an inch of its life most Sundays.

Anne Partridge wanted to know about *piano* lessons, of course she did. It is funny what hearsay can do, isn't it? I tell one person, my next-door neighbour, that I used to play the odd concert hall and next thing I know there's knocking at my door. Well, perhaps it was that delightful fragrance, maybe it was that whisper-blond hair of hers, and that perfect, white smile, but I caved in and agreed for them to come to my house the following Saturday so I would give each of her children a lesson—for a good fee, of course. A young woman might work enchantments on me, but not to the extent that I lose my business sense, I'll have you know.

And so it was young Chloe and her older brother Tim who I was to give lessons to that first Saturday. Both children arrived, as most children do at that age, on a wave of indifference. I noted that same peach fragrance lingering over the both of them, and I thought about how their mother must've busied herself over Tim's bowtie, getting it tied right—because it wasn't one of those which is simply elastic—and on how their mother must've worked on young Chloe's hair that morning. Why, Chloe's hair reminded me of a well-buffed poodle, all curly—the way it had been tucked beneath a band. Anyway, so the children stood there, all ready for their lesson, before me.

Nothing much happened in that first lesson, which is to say that both children looked on at me with complete indifference as I taught them the C major scale and then led them through the first steps of how to play **Ba-Ba Black Sheep**. They trudged out of my house just as soon as I let them go—but not before Tim had handed me over the fee for the lesson, in cash, as I always take it.

As I stood by my door, pulling my pipe out from where it sat on the ledge and thumbing in a fresh clump of tobacco, I watched the children slouch off along the street, neither speaking to the other. I could see, just beyond them, to their house at the end of the street. As I held a match to my pipe I caught movement out of the corner of my eye—the front door of the Partridge door opening up.

I puffed out my first lungful of smoke, savouring that earthy, ashen taste on the way back out, and then I saw Mrs Partridge—Anne—appear in the narrow slither of the doorway. Now, I must admit at this point, whatever my personal feelings toward Anne —her attractiveness to me—I knew full well that she would never be interested in someone like me, and in any case she was married. And so I blew out another few puffs of smoke, thinking of waving to her by way of greeting before turning back inside.

When I did catch her eye the problem was that I couldn't look away.

As she peered out from her front door, I remember quite clearly grasping the railing at the edge of my flowerbeds and curling my fingers around it—feeling its coldness and the light *scratch* of my fingernails against its surface. Because, there, quite distinctly even from my distance, standing at my front door and looking down half a street, I could see that maroon-coloured patch on her cheek.

That bruise.

For the longest time, her holding the front door open, the children slowly, grudgingly making their way back along the road —both their backs to me—she eyed me, no trace of a smile on her lips. As the children reached the concrete steps which led up to their door, she shifted her focus away from me, pinning on a smile as she turned to look at the children.

I took one long suck on my pipe, tipped out the remainders of the ash on my doorstep and then headed back inside. I recall hearing the *thud* of the Partridge house door closing before I closed my own.

2

A FTER THAT LITTLE INCIDENT I took it upon myself —unconsciously or consciously, I'm not quite sure—to keep an extra special eye out on the Partridges. In fact, and this strikes me as a little odd, sounding a little *obsessed*, thinking about it now, I kept a notebook on their comings and goings, perhaps with half a mind to calling up the police at some point, to make some comment if it was required.

Oh those first few days there really wasn't much to comment on. Being retired, or at least semi-retired, I find that I spend most of my time at home now, and so I can say with near certainty that I was on hand to track any activities happening on the street. And with my mind as intrigued as it was I found myself turning the radio down quiet, even moving my favourite armchair—the one with the flowery design and beautifully upholstered, well-stuffed cushions—so that I could be nearer my front door, so that I had an unobstructed view out to the Partridge house.

I noted, in my notebook, when Adam Partridge would go to work in the morning, taking the children along with him and, I suppose, dropping them on the way to school. Although there was another car parked in the drive, I hardly ever saw it missing from the driveway. Well, considering that I was keeping a written record, I can say with near certainty that Anne Partridge never left the house those first few days.

What with the internet being what it is these days, there's not all that much need to leave the house. Just like me it turned out that Anne would order through the same supermarket, that our deliveries would arrive in exactly the same van. That, I have to admit, was when I think I crossed the line, leaving behind the casual note-taking and moving up a notch to making it more of an obsession.

It was odd, kind of an off-the-cuff remark, I don't think that I even thought about the question. There was that pair of *thuds* and I answered the door to the deliveryman, who, for some reason, refuses to use my rather nice brass knocker. He stood there, in the evening chill, hopping from one foot to the other with his electronic device for me to sign. I did just that and I helped him lug those plastic crates into my kitchen, and then dispense the plastic bags about, despite his protests that he didn't want me to break a hip, or something to that effect.

I didn't think to remark on his insufferably bad breath or body odour, but then some of us have a little more decorum . . . if not modesty.

On his way out I remember listening to him groan a little as he piled up those plastic crates and pad out across my carpets in those hefty boots of his, on the way to the front door. As I usually do, I was reading through the machine printout of my order, checking over the items that they hadn't been able to locate at the warehouse and the amendments they'd made on my order where a suitable replacement could be found. I had only skipped down through the first few items before I noticed that this certainly wasn't my receipt.

My mind put it all together quickly. I knew that it must be the Partridges and I was on the cusp of calling out to the delivery-man, calling him back to tell him of his error, when I noticed that, beneath the Partridges' printout, was mine. After a quick sequence of deduction, I decided that the deliveryman would arrive at the Partridge house, have no receipt for them, but neither would he have my receipt, and thus have no *real* means of knowing where the Partridges' was—where the mix up had taken place.

And so I stayed quiet and laid the Partridges' receipt on the side counter, waiting to see if the deliveryman returned.

He didn't.

3

I SPENT most of that evening going through their list, taking in the various items. There wasn't anything at all revelatory, just the normal things, things that families buy: the breakfast cereals, the shampoos and soaps, and so on. Nothing at all noteworthy or remarkable. To tell the truth it made me feel a little sad, made me feel a little nostalgic for the family I'd never had myself. Perhaps I should've thrown the receipt away, but I didn't. Call it what you like, but I folded it into neat quarters and then tucked it inside my notebook for safekeeping.

My notebook remained somewhat dull for the next week or so, only work and school runs. I now kept a plastic, digital wristwatch beside my notebook, pen and pipe on the windowsill. All the times fell within standard ranges, never altering more than fifteen minutes or so either side. Traffic, I supposed. The other car, the light blue hatchback, remained parked up in the drive, unmoved and seemingly unmoving. But, then, there was an *anomaly.*

Once more I was out on my front step, cupping the pleasantly warm chamber of my pipe and feeling that glow pass through me too. It must've been about ten o'clock at night, I'm afraid that— aside from my recordings of the Partridges' daily activities—I've never been too much of a timekeeper. That was when I heard the *scrape* of a key in the lock of the Partridges' front door and then saw Anne's spindly frame emerge.

She was wearing heels, I could tell by the *clack* of her footsteps. Seemingly without noticing me, she got into that hatchback car, switched on the ignition and, after a brief pause, the headlights blinked on, setting the street in a kind of artificial twilight.

I breathed out the blue pipe smoke, perhaps as a way of letting her know she was being watched—again if it was intentional I have no way of recalling—and as I stared through that mist of mine, I watched her drive along the road, before coming to a stop at the bottom of the steps leading up to my front door.

She seemed a little hurried, her mascara smudged, hair less than immaculate. And yet, even through my breathed-out smoke, over the stench of the car exhaust, I caught a whiff of that peachy perfume. As she spoke to me she kept both of her hands fixed on the steering wheel and kept looking back over her shoulder as if someone might be perusing her—Adam Partridge, I supposed. Her voice, though, that stayed firm and sure. Ladylike.

"Mr Joones," she said. "I'm afraid that the children won't be able to take piano lessons anymore."

I smiled lightly and held my pipe down by my side, so as not to lose a single sniff of that perfume of hers. "Oh," I said. "That's a shame."

Although I felt just the opposite.

She glanced back over her shoulder, into the backseat of the car, and then snapped back around to me. "I'm going away for a while," she said. "I . . . I . . . ." but then her words were just smothered in sobs.

Well, I could hardly stand there doing nothing, could I? So I took a step toward the car, putting on a look of concern. "Is something the matter, Mrs Partridge?"

She looked up at me and then forced a smile. It just made her look more manic, more terrified than before. I could see the bruise on her cheek had faded slightly—perhaps she had attempted to cover it with layer upon layer of concealer—but it was most definitely still there.

I decided that that was the point to admit what I'd seen, to play the conscientious neighbour. "Mrs Partridge," I began.

"No," she said, cutting me off, "I'm quite all right, it's just that me and Adam, we've had a bit of a falling out. I'm going to stay away for a while—going to stay with my mother."

I think I can still feel the heat in my cheeks from that blush.

She gave me another forced smile, wound up the window and then drove off into the night, leaving only a mist of exhaust and the fading high-pitched *hum* of the hatchback's engine in her wake.

Anne Partridge didn't return.

4

I KEPT AN EYE OUT on the Partridge house, but for me at that stage I must admit that the thrill of the whole thing had pretty much gone. I kept up the notebook entries, rather half-heartedly, continuing to fill in the comings and goings of Adam and the children, watching their huddled forms in the larger estate car rumble along the street every morning. Often in the evenings, as if expecting something to happen, I would rest up against the cold metal railing and puff away on my pipe, gazing off into the middle distance, hoping for something to distract me.

It was during one of those long, drawn-out waits on the steps, and I think—considering it now—some remnant of that peachy perfume on the stiff autumn breeze, that I came to the realisation that I could be more than just an observer: a voyeur. Maybe it was during one of the dozen times I looked over that shopping list, those normal family items they had purchased—the sting of the past, lost forever, can be an extremely potent one. But I reached the conclusion that it should fall to me to help reunite this couple, help them see sense, that they wouldn't live forever, that if they kept up this fight between the two of them—this *separation*—they might end up just like me.

And so, this idea in mind, one evening having seen Adam Partridge pull into the house after work, I picked up the phone and dialled the number which Anne had left for me, so that during one of the children's piano lessons I might call with any problems. I rang several times without answer, getting through to the voicemail each time. I remember feeling the plastic handset warming in my grip, and telling myself that I would just leave the whole thing right there, step back, stop being such a nosy neighbour. But every time I resolved not to ring again, I found my finger slipping onto the redial button and the whole drama would play out again. And again. Until I heard the other end click and husky breathing in my ear. I could almost taste Adam Partridge's cologne, his manly breath, perhaps just recently eaten and settling down by the fire with a newspaper clutched in his hands —I always imagined the Partridges having an open, wood-burning fireplace.

I had the funny sensation, no more than a slight tingle, that I might be disturbing him. And I thought of hanging up right away. Only then did I remember that the phones—phones nowadays—have all manner of caller identification services, and so I stayed on the line, took a deep breath then said, "This is Patrick Joones, the piano teacher, I taught your children—Tim and Chloe a while ago."

There was a long pause on the other end of the line, a little scuffling. When Adam spoke it was with a weary voice. "Oh yes, I remember."

"Right," I said, beginning to sweat, already damning my involvement in this whole affair and thinking of an escape plan. And yet, I decided that I had to get it out. I had to tell this thing straight, how I saw it.

"Mr Partridge," I continued, "I hope you'll forgive my nosiness, but I couldn't help noticing that yourself and Mrs Partridge have had something of a, well, I should say a falling out." I cleared my throat. "You see, I had an encounter with her, while she was on her way out of the house—leaving in her hatchback, you see. Said that she was going to stay with her mother."

Now I was sweating profusely and heat was rising into my cheeks. I got a sour taste of tobacco in my mouth and rubbed it into my gums with my tongue. This had been such a silly idea, completely nuts really. I had no idea what sort of opinion Adam Partridge was forming of me then, but I continued, knowing I couldn't hang up now. "All I wanted to say was that . . . well, that there's really . . . I . . . I'm a lonely man and, although just an observer, I can tell you with great experience and a weight of confidence that if there's a chance, uh, any chance, of yourself and Mrs Partridge reconciling, you should grasp it with both hands."

Out of nowhere I felt a lump form in my throat. I swallowed it back and blinked rapidly, trying to rid the tears building in my eyes. "Take it from me. You—neither of you—wants to reach my age alone. So, please, whatever it may be that's keeping the two of you apart, I *urge* you to fix the problem. It'll be for the best, I promise."

I waited for the reply, picturing Adam Partridge in his front hall, grasping the telephone to his ear, no doubt with a wrinkled brow, staring off into empty space, wondering just how this call had popped up out of nowhere.

After about ten seconds of silence, I decided I needed to prompt him to speak. "Mr Partridge," I said. "Would you excuse my nosiness?"

Another brief pause, and then, "Thank you, Mr Joones. Really. Thank you."

I waited for something else, but it appeared that that was all I was going to get. And so I took it upon myself to wish him a good night, to apologise once again for my impertinence, and to beg his forgiveness.

Then I hung up.

5

I SUPPOSE that phone call should've scratched my itch, moved my mind onto other things. There was a piano concerto that I'd been in the midst of writing just that afternoon which needed finishing, but I just couldn't bring myself to scrub the matter from my mind. So it was with unquiet thoughts that I went to bed that night and, like always, failed to find sleep until the early hours.

It wasn't until another night, sometime later, and with no sign of Anne Partridge returning, that I plucked up the courage to steal out of my house—again just after I'd seen Adam Partridge coming home from work in his estate—and actually found myself padding up those steps and ringing the Partridges' doorbell.

I glanced in through the frosted glass in the front door, seeing a dim light from within. I stared inside, trying to make sense of the dark shapes. I thought I could see a hat stand, off to the left, the beginning of the staircase to the right, and, in front, another doorway which might lead to the kitchen, or a sitting room perhaps.

I rang several times, unable to obtain a response. I knew that Adam Partridge was there, inside the house, and that he was ignoring me. And, to tell the truth, I knew that I was being impertinent, and that I needed to stop this all-out obsession.

But I just couldn't.

I remember sitting on a stool in my kitchen, listening to my heart beating in my eardrums, and thinking, thinking about the Partridges. Those *damn* Partridges, I just couldn't shake them out of my head. Just when I was reaching the end of my wick, wanting to drink a quarter of gin to get my mind clean, I heard that familiar pair of dual *thumps* on my door. I opened up to, of course, find the deliveryman standing there.

And I had my answer.

It took a touch of convincing, a little white lie, to get myself along with the deliveryman, bringing that receipt from so long ago—telling him that I'd just that moment realised my mistake, and feigning a touch of elderly over-concern, insisted that I accompany him right then and there to their door so that the deliveryman himself wouldn't get in trouble for the undelivered receipt from weeks before.

I stood there with him on the doorstep to the Partridges' house taking in that familiar body odour, that coffee-scented breath of the deliveryman, and I resisted the temptation to light up my pipe which was nestled in the pocket of my jacket, a means to calm my shaking hands. He thumped several times before there was any sound of movement from within the house. And then, wonder of all wonders, I listened to the *creak* of hinges as the door opened up.

It wasn't Adam Partridge who darkened the doorway, though, but Anne.

My breath caught in my throat and I almost tumbled backward, so overwhelming it was to see her face after all this time— as sure as I'd been that she'd long gone to her mother's house. And then a deep happiness, euphoria for the Partridges, that they'd somehow managed to make things work.

But I had to know more.

However, she reacted not at all to me, looking only to the deliveryman, signing his electronic device before accepting the delivery. I attempted to speak with her but she ignored me totally, and, believing that I truly had become invisible, I stepped over the threshold, receipt clutched in my fist.

Anne Partridge acknowledged me then. She flashed her eyes at me in a way I'd never before seen. "*What* do you want?"

I got caught up by shaking and I found myself thrusting the

receipt toward her, muttering something or other under my breath, an apology no doubt.

She whipped the paper from my hand and read it over, then she looked up at me expectantly, now a slight smile on her lips. "You . . . you *took* this, didn't you?"

I was lost for words.

"Yes," she said. "I know just what you did." She took a step toward me, her peachy perfume just as thick as ever, her face delicate—like a china doll's. "Don't think I haven't seen you, on those steps, *watching* the house." She sniffed a slight laugh. "That notebook you keep on your window ledge, I saw that too."

Just then the deliveryman slunk back into the hallway. He looked between the both of us, then forced a smile, weaved his way between us and headed out through the door to his van.

We stood in silence while we listened to the *thrum* of the engine starting up.

When Anne Partridge spoke again it was with bile. "Get out of my house."

Again, I was caught by a series of shudders, feeling numbness creeping across my skin. I found myself taking steps backwards, heading out of the house. And, before I could think about what was happening, I felt the *whoosh* of the air on my face and the *slam* of the door resonate right to the base of my gums.

I was caught in two minds. There was the unchecked delight about the Partridges, that somehow they had seen past their difficulties and moved on, and then there was Anne Partridge's reaction to me. I guess the only way to describe it might be something approaching heartbreak.

It seems silly—*wild*—to consider it now, but I suppose I had something of a *crush* on her.

I pulled my pipe from my pocket and stuck it between my lips, easing my tongue into the well-worn dip in the stem, treating it as some form of comfort blanket. I lit a match and held it over the chamber, waiting for the tobacco to light, sucking at the stem as I tried to convince it to do so. And then, as I looked up through my first exhale of smoke, to the estate car sitting there in the driveway, I saw them, the two children.

In the backseat.

I stared for a long time into those sallow faces looking out from under glass, both of them wrapped up tight in their winter coats, scarves stuffed into the necks of their jackets, all dressed in their school uniforms.

I stood rooted to the spot unable to believe those glassy eyes —that those glassy eyes were real, that they hadn't been fixed there as part of some taxidermy job. I glanced back up at the Partridges' house, and then, seeing no one looking out from the windows, I approached the car.

There was no doubt.

The children were dead.

6

BACK HOME I puffed away, no longer caring about my smoking inside. I watched the smoke linger up into my kitchen's bright yellow lights and tried to think. I knew that I should've called the police, that I should've told them right away, but it was the book, that *damn* notebook, I was ashamed, was worried about what they'd think of me. It wasn't until the nascent light of dawn shone blue on the horizon that I plucked up the courage to hit the Call button, to put myself through to the police.

They came at once, silent in the early morning, only the gentle ticking of their blue lights violating the calm. And I stood on my front step as they brought Anne Partridge out of the house, in handcuffs, led her down to the waiting backseat of the car.

The policeman's questions came and went, like a lapping tide, and I found myself spilling all the details, trying to get everything in order so as to help with their inquiries as best I could.

In a way it felt nice to purge all of those pent-up secrets, to hand over the notebook of the Partridges' comings and goings for use in the case.

And that was where my involvement with the matter reached an end, the rest of my connection was merely through newspaper reports, following the development of the investigation. I found that I got the story in snippets. That the car—the hatchback—containing her husband had been found dumped into a stream, alcohol in his system, stab marks in his chest. How Anne Partridge had killed the children, too, and then, dressed up in her husband's suit, gone through the daily routine of driving them along in the estate, as if headed to work, dropping the kids off at school.

She had got away with it for weeks and weeks.

And I had just stood and stared like some dumbstruck idiot.

I suppose it just goes to show that even us curtain twitchers have some use. Even if they don't know it themselves.

Well, at least I saw the man in the murderer.

Eventually.

POLAR HELL

1

I CAN HEAR the melted snow dripping onto canvas. We're still here. Although, I dreamt we wouldn't be.

I zip back the tent flap and peer out into the whiteness. Completely white. How could anything survive here? The answer is it can't. Not without making itself more aggressive, more devastating and more deadly than the environment itself.

We should have taken it as an omen when our flight was delayed by six days. The engineer found a mouse nesting inside the circuitry. It bit through a large amount of wires looking for food for its babies. It surprised the engineer it didn't bite off anything which would've blown it straight to hell. Lucky mouse.

Here we are in the tundra. Nothing but snow.

2

ORIGINALLY THERE WERE six of us: me, my brother Brian, my father and his three friends. Here on holiday; my father's idea of holiday.

"This is nothing!" he said, at the start of the trip.

The man who prided himself on climbing The Seven Summits: the seven highest peaks on the seven continents. I suppose that was what led him to this adventure, the only continent my father had yet to set foot on.

Well, here we are, Daddy. The Arctic!

3

I STEP OUT of the tent. My snowshoes crunch as I put my foot down in fresh snow.

I look out across the scene, making a tunnel with my hands over my eyes to shield them from the sun.

I'd like to say that today is a new day but the truth is I have no idea. The last time the beast struck we had to run, leaving behind my father—and the GPS—to save our own skins. For all I know I've been in that tent five minutes. Although I hope not because I'd like to live to see my twenty-fifth birthday, which might or might not be today.

Behind me there's a cough. I spin round, any stray sound in this echo chamber pulls at my attention.

I relax.

My brother, Brian, emerges from the tent.

"What took you so long?" I say.

He squints at me with big bags under his eyes.

I turn back to the face the landscape. "What do we do now?"

"Walk towards the sun," he says.

I shake my head. "Is that the best you've got?"

He shrugs and bends down to get something from inside the tent.

4

MY YOUNGER BROTHER. I've looked out for him ever since he was this tall.

I remember the day I pulled him out of the rowing boat, the one he got for his eighth birthday. He'd pushed himself off, the blue birthday ribbon still tied to the hull, way out into the middle of the lake. I stood on the bank, with my mother and father, watching him slip across the water.

"Look after your brother," Mum had said. "We'll be back soon." They set off in the car to the shop, about fifteen miles down a dirt track.

When I returned to the lake I didn't see him. I ran up and down the bank screaming out his name but no response came. I thought of my father's advice.

I stopped, took a deep breath and let my mind wander for a solution. Then I knew that he'd drifted off, downstream.

I raced in the direction of the current. Soon the tranquil lake evolved into rushing rapids. The noise filled my ears as I rushed past trees, scraping my arms on the branches.

I peeked out from between a pair of pine trees to see the wreckage of my brother's boat spread across the frothing water and up the banks.

My heart stopped.

As I ran down to the river the sharp rocks cut at the bare soles of my feet. I reached the riverside to see my brother lying facedown in a small puddle to one side of the river.

I flipped him over and pushed down on his chest, perhaps recalling something I saw on TV (I wouldn't take a First Aid course until a couple of years later).

His eyes fluttered and he turned over with a blank expression on his face. He was so blue I thought he was a corpse.

We didn't tell my mother and father what happened that day. They didn't return until much later. When they asked about the boat my brother told them he forgot to harness it to the port. My father scolded him but my mother's eyes told a different story. She smelled the lie.

Perhaps I should feel sad about my father's death. But, the truth is, he was never there.

Shortly after that eventful eighth birthday party my parents got divorced and my father went to live in Asia. We don't know where exactly. He never talked about it. Then he started to climb mountains.

5

"**H**EY, LOOK!" Brian waves a package at me. "I found an energy bar."

My stomach grumbles.

"Do you want it?" he says.

"Nah, it's for you."

Sometimes I hate playing the older brother. My father used to tell me helping others can get you killed. I suppose he talked about situations like this one.

"Sure?"

I smile. "Yeah."

His wide eyes move away from me to the energy bar, packed full of sugar and vitamins. As I watch him eat I consider whether that was the last decision I'll get to make on Earth.

Half an hour later we pack up the tent and continue beating the path to God-knows-where.

I head up the expedition while my brother lags behind. I tell him to hurry up and he obliges, drawing up alongside me. We walk together in silence for what must be two kilometres.

"Dan?"

"Yeah?" I inch my thumbs under the backpack straps so that they don't cut into my shoulders.

"Where're we going?"

"Home."

"But, we don't have a compass."

I stop dead in my tracks. "Would you like to lead us off?"

Brian considers and his face contorts into a frown. "No."

"Right then, let's crack on then, shall we?"

More silence as we trudge through the tundra looking for signs of anything at all. In this place with the biting cold and shifting path under my feet I find it difficult to keep my mind tethered up. It drifts. Phrases such as, 'I saw a man die,' slip through my brain and repeat over and over again.

Watching a man die is much worse than just seeing a corpse. I know because I've experienced both. I suppose the corpse shocked me, being the first time I saw a dead person, but the screams and the sight of seeing someone killed just doesn't compare.

We'd pitched the tents in a U-shape by a large rock, to break the north wind. I emerged from the tent and what I saw in front of me made my bones shudder.

My heart leapt to my throat and beat wildly, as if it would burst out of me and onto the pristine white floor in a crimson puddle.

He lay face down, that was how I knew he was dead. You don't lie facedown in the snow, not in the Arctic. Not for fun.

My father poked his head out of the tent. He said something like, "Hey, what's taking so long?" His words remained answered and they blew away on a stiff breeze.

I don't remember him saying anything to me, not directly. But I do remember going back inside my tent and zipping up. I lay down on the open sleeping bag. Brian asked me if breakfast was ready and I told him, "No, not yet."

He didn't ask any more questions that day.

Heart attack. Unfortunately, we had no way to inform his family. Terry was his name. We'd only met a couple of days earlier. We buried him at noon the same day he died in the fresh snow.

Although I'm religious or anything it would've been nice to have put him into the ground, into dirt. Tradition dies hard.

That afternoon we decided to go home, to give up the expedition. Death strips the fun out of everything.

I almost laugh when I think back to the conversations we had, at the beginning, travelling from the main camp out onto the tundra.

I remember Patrick, another of my father's friends, saying, "Not much ice here, is there? Must be impossible for the bears to get around."

Soon lost among the other comments, it remained drifting around my head. I don't think he would've said it with a smile on his face if he'd known that within seventy-two hours he'd be inside one of those bears.

6

S OMETHING RUMBLES BEHIND US.
I duck instinctively.

When nothing happens I look around me, still in a crouched position, to see what made the noise. To my right a large amount of snow falls down the cliff. The powder rises from the place where it dropped. It's like cannon smoke.

We surrender.

7

THAT NIGHT, or what my father's GPS claimed was night —the sun never sets here, not in summer—we pitched in at the side of the sea. Although we were making good progress on our way back to the main camp, a morbid air had set in over the group—so distant from the high-spirits that accompanied the start of the adventure.

At around midnight I heard one of those familiar horror film lines: "I'll be back in a minute," Patrick had said.

The tent zipped shut and I listened as he paced away from the campsite, in search of a suitable location to urinate.

Funny that his politeness, or his want for privacy, cost him his life. Me and Brian speculated later that the bear was just passing by, probably fishing, and Patrick proved too tempting.

A shrill scream brought me round from my light sleep.

Outside the sun continued to shine. It didn't take much to raise everyone from their sleep. Here it's impossible to get the sound sleep darkness allows.

When I opened the tent flap I saw my father and Graham running from the camp in the direction of the noise. They returned even faster.

"Pack up the tents!" my father said. "Let's go!"

The blind panic pushed me into action. We had no idea what was wrong.

Brian turned back to look and my father had to pull him round so he wouldn't be left behind like a stray sheep lost in the fog—left to the mercy of those fangs and claws.

8

I STOP DEAD.

Brian bumps into me from behind. "Hey," he says. "What's going on?"

I glance at him, his face pale. He meets my eye and both of us fix our eyes to the floor. We examine the tracks. Fresh prints, leading all the way to the horizon or so it seems.

"Did you see where they started?" I say.

"No, I would've told you if I had."

I push my tongue up to the roof of my mouth where I pause to feel the ridges. A nervous habit I picked up in school.

"So which way do we go?" Brian looks around constantly, as if the bear could sneak up behind us unseen.

I bend down to the snow and look at the prints. If the bear finds us here, in clear sight, we will die. And if I choose wrong, go in the direction the bear's heading, we'll die too.

"Which way was the bear going?" Brian says.

I look in both directions along the tracks. "This way." I try to sound convincing and in control but I don't know if he believes me. He follows anyway. He'd probably follow me all the way to hell.

9

THE NIGHT AFTER the bear killed Patrick we bedded down in a cave. We were all starving, having hiked as fast as possible out of fear.

I began to re-examine my father. This man conquered great snowy peaks, swam through jungles and laughed in the faces of cannibals. Or so he said. Seeing his face filled with panic frightened me.

The glowing blue light from the gas stove lit up the cave.

"Dad?" I said.

"Yeah?"

"Why did you leave Mum?"

He didn't sigh and make an excuse to leave, as he almost always did; nowhere for him to go. He looked back at me through his four-day-old stubble and smiled. "Dan," he said. "Life will pass you by if you're not careful."

I frowned. "What does that have to do with anything?"

"How old are you?"

"Twenty-four."

He nodded and said, "You wouldn't understand, then."

"Try me."

He shook his head and looked at the flame, which sent an array of dancing shadows up and down the walls.

"Please, Dad, was it another woman?"

He smirked and remained silent.

"Then why?"

My father kept the same neutral smile on his face. "You'll find out when you're older, son."

Brian poked his head out from our tent. He pulled his bulk out through the flap and, crawling on hands and knees, sat alongside us. "What's up? You guys talking woke me up."

And that was the end of the 'serious' conversation.

Jason, my father's remaining friend, either didn't hear us or was too polite to break the tension because he stayed in his tent. Perhaps Patrick and Terry's deaths had hit him harder than he'd let on. I'll never know.

For me it was less of a big deal. I mean, once I got over the initial shock. How much can you feel for someone you only met yesterday?

The next day we would've arrived back at the base camp. All we had to do was walk in a straight line.

10

"SHIT!" I SAY.

It starts under my breath but the sharp 't' sound sneaks out at the last moment as I fail to hold my frustration inside. I kick at a snow drift.

"Jesus!" Brian says, as he turns the corner to join me, seeing it for himself.

We walked up a steady slope in the past hour, hoping it would lead to a better vantage point—to see where we should be going. But now we've reached the edge of the cliff and all around us the Arctic sea spreads. Grey as far as the eye can see, and then white beyond that.

I look out over the sea. "Nothing."

"What's that?" Brian says, pointing and squinting.

I look to where he points and my heart skips a beat.

An object, about a hundred metres away, appears as discoloured grey against the crisp white snow. It bounds towards us, its four powerful legs propelling the enormous jaws forward.

"Get down!" I pull Brian to the ground and we watch in silence as the bear comes closer.

On our viewing platform we sit around ten metres above the bear. That distance won't make much difference—*any* difference —if it spots us.

I look around for options but, with the sea to one side and a natural born killer on the other, there's no way out.

No way out.

11

I DON'T REMEMBER exactly when Jason fell behind the rest of us. I guess we'd walked for three or four hours when he disappeared. We stopped and shouted out to him but after over an hour of searching we decided to move on—too dangerous to hang about with the clouds coming in and a bear nosing his way along our trail.

We broke for lunch by the Arctic sea. Seeing the storm come in, we decided to put the tent up.

We sat around the gas stove with the heat bouncing off the walls and enveloping us in comfort. The wind bent the sides of the tent into our bodies and the sea pounded the shore a few hundred metres away. We leant into each other for heat. I imagine each of our faces looked grim.

"Any chance of a cup of tea?" Brian had whispered.

"I think so," my father said. He swung his bag round so it sat between us.

I watched my father's hands shake as he struggled with the zip. I looked at his face. It remained brave, his mouth forced into a smile and the tip of his tongue poking out. He dropped the box of tea bags onto the mat.

"What're you going to tell their families, Dad?" Brian said.

My father paused in his preparations. "I don't know," he said. "I haven't thought about it."

We sat in silence. I saw the cogs turning just beneath the skin of my father's forehead. His fellow expatriates, his best friends for the past ten, fifteen years and he didn't give anything away.

12

W E SHIVERED through the night. The storm refused to let off for a second. The closest it had got to darkness during our Arctic stay.

I unzipped the tent and poked my head outside in the midst of the storm. The wind and hail buffeted me back inside.

My father had to help pull the zip closed as the two sides of the tent flapped wildly together.

I sank back on my sleeping bag and watched my father's chest rise and fall. I realised he wasn't a young man anymore, no longer the vital and strong hero of my youth. His cheeks flushed red from the cold and his hair seemed thinner and wirier than I'd noticed before. "Dad? Are you ok?"

He turned to me and attempted to smile, to let me know that everything was ok. However, as the corners of his mouth tightened he leaned forward and flew into a coughing fit.

I thought he was going to choke to death on his own phlegm. It took both me and Brian to pull him straight. I smacked him on the back and tried to loosen whatever sat in his throat.

He fell back into our arms, his eyes closed, and slipped into sleep.

B ELOW US the bear paces, back and forth, as if in a zoo.
I squeeze Brian to my body, to keep him from breathing. Perhaps the bear won't smell us.

The bear pads down to the shore, its coat glimmering in the sun. I see the dried blood on its chest, the dirty brown colour.

The bear submerges its head in the water.

We lie still.

The bear's head emerges, snapping to one side. A fish drops on the snow. It sits back, on his bottom, reminding me of a teddy bear I used to have when I was a kid.

I laugh hysterically.

Brian jabs me in the ribs. "Shh!" he says. "Are you crazy?"

I cover my mouth with my hand to stop more hysterics slipping out.

The bear sits there, looking at the fish—all the time reminding me of the teddy. Just a silly, harmless stuffed teddy. The fish flaps up and down off the ground but the bear remains in the same place watching its death dance. And then his paw whips out, catching the fish on its head, and the fish stops jumping.

14

AT FIRST I thought it was the silence that woke me. I propped myself up on my elbows and rubbed the couple hours' sleep from my eyes. I listened carefully.

The wind had dropped and the hail had ceased. The storm had stopped. The gentle lapping of the waves was the only sound outside.

Brian and my father slept soundly at my side.

When I lay back down, that was when I heard the rustling.

The unmistakable sound of footsteps trudging through snow.

Jason, I thought.

I untangled myself from the sleeping bag, knocking the other two several times.

They slept on, oblivious.

I brought my winter jacket around my shoulders and zipped it up to my neck. In the tent porch I pulled on my boots and ventured outside into the bright sunshine.

I got to my feet unsteadily, after lying down so long I felt a little wobbly. I surveyed the terrain.

A shape on the horizon caught my eye. Was it moving?

I bent down to the tent and screamed out in warning.

When my father and Brian emerged, the bear was close—perhaps a hundred metres away.

We ran as fast as we could.

I glanced back several times over my shoulder to see the bear trot closer to the tent. When he reached it he sniffed around, entered one of them. I remember his off-white bottom facing us as he nuzzled around inside.

We got about halfway across the tundra, halfway towards the cover of the caves, when the panting, the lolloping *pad* of footsteps made me turn.

The bear was bounding towards us at top speed.

My mouth tried to make a sound but the whistling wind took it away. But I only needed to look at my father and Brian's faces to see that they were screaming too.

My survival instincts took over and I disregarded the fierce cold and uneven surface to run for my life.

The regular pants of my father and Brian followed me, along with the relentless *pad* of paws on packed snow.

A scream pierced the air, striking me like an arrow.

Brian rushed towards me.

Beyond, I saw the bear's front paws pinning my father to the ground by his chest. My father wrestled back against it, like in a movie.

I felt a strong urge to run but I remained transfixed. The first sign of blood, seeping from my father's arm, brought me back to reality, and I knew what it was I had to do. "Come on!" I said, pulling at Brian's arm.

He stood firm.

I took his resistance as shock but when I tugged at him a second time I saw the expression on his face—disgust. "We can't leave him. He's our Dad."

"Of course we can. We have to save ourselves!"

Brian didn't answer my question. He took a couple of steps towards the battle scene. I held him back.

"Let me go!" he said.

"No, you're not going to kill yourself, too!" I grabbed his wrist and looked into his eyes. "This was his choice. The life he chose."

"The bag!" Brian tried to break free from my grasp.

I saw he wanted to point out the rucksack which lay to my father's side.

The tent, I thought. Any chance of survival we had rested on retrieving it. I ran past Brian and towards man and bear, the life and death struggle taking place.

Blood seeped onto the snow—crimson on bridal white.

Growling sounds came from the two of them. My father held his own against the bear but it was clear that there would only be one winner in the end.

I pushed my arm through one of the bag straps. I took a final look at the fight: predator and prey. Dad caught my eye.

At first I thought it was the bear making the deep guttural growl but then I saw that it was my father's lips that moved. "Go," he said. "Go!"

Those words followed me as a kind of mantra as I beat my way back towards Brian.

Go, go, go—

Crunch.

And then silence.

The hair on my neck stood on end.

Tears streamed down Brian's face, freezing, leaving a trail from the corners of his eyes right down to his chin.

We ran.

15

THE BEAR eats the fish. It holds it to its mouth with its paw. Is this the appetiser or dessert? It finishes, licking his lips. Then it sits washing itself, like a cat.

We sit tight, waiting.

The bear looks around. Does it have the feeling it's being watched?

I squeeze my eyes shut and hope that when it finds us it'll kill us quickly, not play with us. Surely, he's had enough to eat, now. Surely?

I shake but not from the cold. My warm winter jacket keeps out the biting chill.

The bear moves from its spot. It pauses a moment, as if making a decision, and then, apparently decided, heads back to the tundra: the lone hunter, striding out.

It warms me inside.

We don't speak until the bear is a speck on the great white canvas. We look at each other and then embrace. We should be dead. My brother's body warmth is my last connection to home, my last comfort.

"Let's get the tent pitched," I say.

Brian nods and drops the rucksack to the ground.

God knows what we're going to do now. No GPS. No map. No hope. Our final option: a message in a bottle.

So, here we are stuck in this polar hell.

Please send help.

LIFE'S LITTLE MISERIES

1

N OTHING MUCH gets done on Sinewy Island.
And certainly not much murder.

So imagine my surprise when I was sitting up at my desk of the front room of my peachy-toned, little retirement cottage and heard an icy-cool scream rattling my window frames.

I got myself up out of my plush, spring-loaded, crimson leather chair as soon as I could. I swished my greatcoat onto my shoulders. Ever since my wife died five years ago, that coat of mine has always hung off the back of my chair. She had a real knack for snuffing out any sort of disorder-making habits of mine, and ever since she's been gone I've begun to revert to my old ways. Guess you *can't* teach an old dog new tricks.

And, like that, I left the warmth of my cottage and, to an extent, my retirement.

Because I'd made a point of getting out of my private-detective trade the moment that I'd bought up this place of mine: miles away from anywhere, sea lashing all around, an hour-long boat ride from the mainland when the boat goes at all.

Down on the promenade—not much more than a collection of rusted-up metal railings and battered-in concrete—I breathed in the sharp, salty, chilly breeze blowing off the sea, felt it sting my rosy cheeks. And, my detective's ears acting like a pair of radar dishes, they drew me to those gasping sounds of air leaving lungs for the last time.

I found her down at the bottom of the promenade steps, lying crumpled up in a heap, against a pile of grey rocks, turned silver in the rising moonlight. Her hair was knotted like gnarled rope, and her features like a hundred sores all cut open at once.

Blood.

There was blood, of course.

I could smell *that* too.

That thick, metallic, familiar—*too familiar*—odour.

As I reached out to take hold of her hand, felt her fingers find mine, wrap themselves about my wrist, I looked into her eyes, and I saw the final light leaving them . . . what some might've termed her 'soul.'

Just like that, as easily as blowing out a candle, her life was extinguished.

And, it seemed, Jack Hegarty, PI, was back in business.

THERE'S NO POLICE on Sinewy Island.
No need.

Just about the worst crime ever recorded on the island was the theft of Adam Naughton's dinghy, and even then there's a school of thought which goes that it sailed on off on a stormy night, simply cut itself loose and floated on off.

Till the murder of Marley Evermoore, that was.

And right on my front doorstep.

The list of suspects was short.

Only five other people lived on the island.

And all at least in their sixties, if not older.

Others came and went, of course, some of them relatives of those remaining here. But they were just what was known to us, on the island, as 'day visitors.'

Maybe day visitors spend a night, here and there, but there's no doubt that they wouldn't be capable of the solitude that Sinewy Island demands. They wouldn't have been able to see out a week of autumn gales, let alone a winter of barren, snow-covered hillsides, and no boats coming in till spring.

Not that I blame them.

Sinewy Island is a place for people who've lived.

And who look for shelter.

Away from the world.

And its nastiness.

The next morning, after the murder of Marley Evermoore, the sun shone down, and it was clear. Blue skies opened out above me, setting the verdant hillsides in a healthy glow. As I cycled along down the dirt path, pebbles kicking up in my spokes, I could smell the thick scent of the long grasses on the breeze, and those coupled with the thick odour of the blooming roses all along the lane that Yvonne Hubbard would see to.

I would often slip by and shoot the shit with her husband, Gordon, and he would often be glad to see me, be there waiting with a glass of ale, a sturdy, wooden garden chair sat opposite his own, and nothing but the sea stretching away from us and into the distance.

Today, though, I wasn't here to shoot the shit with Gordon.

I was here to find out who had done Marley Evermoore in.

As I freewheeled my way along the stone wall, which marked the perimeter of the Hubbards' property, I took in their noble, graceful, slate cottage, along with its off-white walls. I remember the first time that I came to Sinewy Island and saw the Hubbards' cottage. I can remember thinking—*wishing*—that just maybe that was the one that I'd been told about, the cottage on the island that was for sale.

No such luck, though, which isn't to say that my own place, my own cottage, is anything at all to be sniffed at.

No, in retrospect, it's just fine for me.

The Hubbards' place would've been far too big for a retired widower, sort of cumbersome, like lugging a tombstone on a thick rope about my neck.

And I had no real desire to lug a tombstone anywhere.

I set my bike leaning up against the side of the cottage, and then knocked on the racing green front door of the Hubbards' cottage. When Yvonne invited me in for tea, I thought it only my place to let her know straightaway what had gone on—what we were dealing with here.

Yvonne, of course, wanted to phone up the police, back on the mainland, wanted to bring them out here. But I knew better. I knew that they wouldn't want to waste time. And what with them being a whole bunch of country bumpkins they'd no doubt end up having to call in somebody from the Big City to come and sort things out properly . . . though not before they'd gone and put those always messy fingerprints of theirs over just about everything.

No, I'd dealt with small town cops in my time, and I had no intention of doing so again.

After all, I most likely had more expertise when it came to murder than even those fancy Big City police that they'd call in.

Yvonne took some calming, and luckily I had Gordon there to side with me.

Sitting out in the Hubbards' back garden, the sun on our faces, the ale cool in its glass, and the wondrous warming sensation of the alcohol ripping through blood, Gordon would often deflect even the slightest of mentions of my previous 'mainland' occupation . . . apparently some gory details cannot be fully comprehended by the mundane.

But, here and now, with this particular case, he made Yvonne see reason.

Made her see my point of view.

We'd surely spoken enough over these years so, even if Gordon didn't precisely understand just what it was I'd got up to in my career, that he did have some sort of confidence in my ability.

That, and me telling the two of them that if we were to have any chance of solving this murder we needed to act quickly, before the murderer—or murderers—had a possibility of making their escape.

They asked me what I'd done with the body.

I told them I'd taken it back to my house—left it in the pantry.

No good for it to sit about on the beach the whole while.

If the country bumpkin police did make it on to our island,

then they'd no doubt contaminate just about everything that they possibly could, so it made little difference who did the contaminating.

We drew up a list of suspects, of the island's residents.

It had got shorter with Marley Evermoore's death, of course.

Only five of us on the island in all.

Now all that remained were myself, Gordon and Yvonne, here with me, Adam Naughton, and then the old widow Dawes who lived up on Dawes Mansion which overlooked the whole island.

Nobody much went on up to Dawes Mansion. No need to. All I knew was, from my years of observations, was that once a month a specially commissioned boat would arrive bearing supplies.

An unmarked van would then ascend the hill, up from the port, and it would carry the shipment to Dawes Mansion before returning to its place: a standalone garage a little way off the beach.

I'd passed the garage a couple of times while taking a walk.

I guessed that the driver and the captain of the boat were one and the same.

I depended on Yvonne and Gordon for most of my knowledge of Dawes Mansion.

Yvonne and Gordon had been living on the island for twenty years. They had both arrived to the island at the commencement of their fifties. And now they were into their seventies. It had been an early retirement plan. Both had been highflying corporate lawyers, and they had plotted their Great Escape for so many years before their chance arrived. And they took it with both hands.

When the two of them had arrived, the only building on the whole of the island had been Dawes Mansion. That elegant, mid-century Victorian mansion perched on top of the hill, and looking so thoroughly out of place on the gloom-ridden island, as if, any day, it might become far too unwieldy for those humble hills and just topple into the sea.

And the frothing waves.

Prior to arriving on the island, Yvonne had purchased just about every book of island history from a shop in the small village of Sesney, back on the mainland, and from which the boats all ran to the island itself.

The island history was mottled with sheep farmers, until they had tired, and then, later on, as a smugglers' cover, till the smugglers had all been rounded up and nobly shot by the king.

And then the Dawes had arrived.

I recalled the first time that Yvonne had described the history of the Dawes Family, and how they had been one of those *very English* old families which had been born with great lands, not to mention wealth, and then gone to such great lengths to lose it all either out of poorly thought-out strategies and investments, or through sheer foolishness.

In the mid-nineteen hundreds the family fortune was a shadow compared to what it had once been. They had debts. Mountains of debts. And the only forthcoming solution, or so it seemed to Lord Dawe, was to sell up the family estate, and the pieces of land, here and there, and to break ground on a new build on Sinewy Island.

Often, while speaking of the Dawes with Yvonne and Gordon, the phrases 'big fish' and 'little pond' cropped up, as if they thought that they might be able to impress themselves on this most natural of domains out in the middle of nowhere.

But I preferred to think of the thing in far different terms.

Because that line of thinking came only from the nouveau riche, and the Dawes may have been many things, but they were —certainly not—nouveau riche.

For me it was not a matter of pride, but a matter of shame.

They wished to hide away.

And a hilltop mansion in the middle of the sea was the only way for them to do it.

The only way for people of *their* means, in any case.

3

YVONNE BROUGHT US our third pot of tea, coupled with a whole array of sugary biscuits which I was sure my doctor, when I returned to the mainland for my yearly check-up, would have tutted and shaken his head at.

The grandfather clock which sat in the corner of their sitting room ticked away to itself, apparently oblivious of the gravity of our conversation.

That murder had taken place.

And here, in the unlikeliest of situations.

A man gets to wondering if death follows on his heels, and where it will all end.

Or if death expects to steal so closely to a man's shadow, playing with him a while before making the fatal, killing stroke.

The sitting room smelled of crushed lavender, and it was very easy to forget the nastiness which had occurred in the early morning simply by allowing myself to sink back into the well-cushioned pillows on the settee. And to allow myself to slip beneath the gentle, warbling tones of Gordon's voice as he rumbled on about this and that, mindless speculations of the uninitiated, those who see murder as a sort of parlour game, as a means to 'pass the time.'

They are the ones who have never stared into the glassy dead eyes of the victims.

And seen the truth.

That there's nothing there.

I sipped on my bitter tea, untouched by any sweetener, and I watched Yvonne back into her own armchair, across from me.

She appeared a little frailer now, juddery *even* . . . reminding me of a highly strung house cat. Her eyes appeared to leap about the room as if making snap judgements here and there. As if an attack might come from any angle and for any purpose.

Hers was the aspect of the one who knows that murder lingers in the shadows, where she had previously been unafraid to tread . . . but which now hung about her neck like a set of lead weights, ready to suck her downwards, into the tarry pit.

"So, Jack" she said, "Do you think it could've been Adam?"

Much was said, I could tell, between Gordon and Yvonne about Adam.

A subsistence fisherman, a man who had, apparently, lived on the island from birth, and who may, or may not, have come over with the first wave of Dawes, ostensibly to aid them but later breaking away from the mother goose, eking out an existence on the cobbled shores of Sinewy.

Less, I could tell, was said between Gordon and Yvonne about myself.

But, then again, in comparison to Adam, I was an open book.

And so goes to show the innocence of the uninvolved, of the regular citizen, of those who I have strived my whole life to escape from, and those who I have found—apparently—tracking me down here to what I hope to be my final resting place.

I gave a shrug. "It's possible."

Gordon turned to me, a slight smile on his creased-up face, his grey beard making him seem far more wizened than I knew him to be. "You can't *seriously* believe that Mrs Dawes could've had something to do with it?"

"We can't rule it out," I said.

Gordon gave me a steely glare, and I felt Yvonne's eyes shifting over me, making me feel uncomfortable, bringing on a deep yearning to escape, to get away from them, to be back among my books, at my desk, etching out my memoirs, staring out to sea.

Trying to observe *her* face in the obscurity.

Trying to find my way home.

I tapped my fingers against my thigh. "Have you ever seen Mrs Dawes out here, down and out of the house, I mean?"

This time it was Yvonne who answered, pulling her cardigan tight about herself as if a chill might've somehow entered the sitting room, though it was set with blazing firelight.

"No," she said, staring into the flames.

"Then how can we deduce that she still lives there, that the Dawes Mansion is really occupied by Mrs Dawes at all?"

They had no answer to my question.

And, in any case, I felt that my work was done with the Hubbards.

I had wanted to come on down to their cottage, had wanted to feel the mood of the place, try to find tension. And I had found it. Ripping through the air. Nothing like the tension I was looking for, though. This tension was a kind of fear. But the sort of fear which only ever comes from the victims, the observers.

I knew, on instinct, that neither of the two of them had had anything to do with the murder of Marley Evermoore.

4

I PEDALLED ON around the coast of the island, noting the way that the clouds had all bunched up on the horizon, and seeing how they had begun to come rolling in over the sea. As I cycled along, feeling the odd stone flick up and strike me on one of my calf muscles, I gazed on up to the Dawes Mansion, watched it in profile as I spun my wheels around it.

And, up there, on the top floor of the place, at the large attic window, I allowed my mind to wander. To see a face up there. Some sort of a ghost story long-ago repressed.

I wondered if it was a built-in trait of all these mansions, every last one of them like a mausoleum, that they were intended to conjure up horrific images in the minds of the living.

As I cycled onwards, I caught sight of Adam's shack.

And it was nothing more than a shack.

What, back on the mainland, would've been little more than a large garden shed.

Outside, drawn up on the rocks, I spied his upturned dingy.

Adam had been out fishing early in the morning—like always.

In the early morning, I would see him fishing out there when I woke, sloshing back and forth among the waves. The bottom of his boat was still slightly damp to the touch. And it smelled strongly of the sea. As I approached the door to his home, he opened up before I even had a chance to knock.

Adam's face was thick with a fuzzy, black beard, and he wore a beanie cap constantly pulled down right to the tips of his bushy eyebrows. His complexion was scarred by the sun and wind, and a ripe stench of body odour and halitosis stuck to him like an invisible swarm of flies. His eyes, like his hair, were black, and humourless, and full of dead sorrow.

He didn't speak so much as grunt.

"Adam?" I said. "Would you mind answering a few questions?"

He regarded me for several seconds before stepping back into his home, apparently inviting me inside.

5

INSIDE THE SHACK, all manner of things hung up on the walls, but, mostly, as far as I could gather, hooks and rods. To be honest, if I hadn't been living on the island for some time—if I'd been one of the much-reviled 'day visitors'—then I might well have found my standing in the place somewhat ominous.

The rotten stench of fish guts clung to everything in the hut, and I could feel the odour stabbing at my guts like a hundred rusted-up knives.

I shallowed my breathing and turned my attention back to Adam who was now darkening the doorway with his silhouette against the ever-dimming, afternoon sky.

When I asked him about that morning, about whether he might've witnessed what had become of Marley Evermoore, he looked away from my eyes. Whereas, back on the job, back in the city, I might well have taken this as a suspicious sign, I knew Adam sufficiently well to realise that this was simply one of his character quirks.

That he simply found the company of other humans some-where between abhorrent and a necessary evil.

Why else did he live out on the coast in this little shack of his?

"A silly woman," Adam said, his voice thick, and husky.

"I'm sorry?" I said, having come into contact with death on often a daily basis in my business, I was still unable to quite gauge *this* particular reaction.

His eyes skirted mine, and then he fixed his attention on some hook, or some rod which hung up in the shadows of his shack. "Hmm, that much was clear, ever since she got here."

I couldn't keep the tone of irritation out of my voice as I said, "I don't follow you."

"Asking questions, going about the island like it was some sort of a place like any other—like she had some kind of a *duty* to understand its history . . . something like that."

I stood there, quite still. I felt a chilly draught sneak into the shack, and I couldn't help wondering how Adam managed to put up with standing about here any length of time, let alone *living* here.

When he looked back at me again, though, his expression was somewhat drier than before, and his features seemed to gain gravity, to become even older. He gave me a stiff nod, and then said, "This morning, they ran her down."

I felt the wrinkles press themselves into my forehead. I stared hard at him through the gloom of the hut, trying to meet his eyes. But they were black and they shifted just as easily as shadows. "What do you mean, 'ran her down?'" I said.

"This morning, that delivery, to the widow Dawes. It came in, right on time."

I thought back to this morning, tried to summon the purring of a boat engine, followed by the gentle rattle of the van I'd grown so used to.

It was true, whenever the widow Dawes received her deliveries, they would often wake me. The van would need to trundle along right past my house, after all.

Could it have possibly woken me that morning?

Had I lain in bed, the scruffy, scratchy blanket pulled up to my neck in a somewhat frail attempt to guard against the fierce morning chill, heard the van rumbling past, dismissed it in some sleepy daze and then turned over and slipped back away to dreamland?

I couldn't recall any van that morning.

I looked deeper into the darkness, tried to burrow into Adam's eyes.

While there was no reason for me not to trust him—at least he had never *given* me a reason—I couldn't help but wonder whether I might have lulled myself into a false sense of security here on the island, had allowed my defences to drop, had failed to spot some evil which dwelled just below the surface.

Could this be Adam's hastily assembled alibi?

As if anticipating my thoughts, Adam continued, "Mrs Dawes, she's a sick lady, you've got to understand that."

I blinked several times, feeling that the darkness was almost as thick and heavy as tar.

"She doesn't leave that house much, not at all, and you being new here, and all"—I supposed that, for Adam, for somebody who might well have been born on the island, that was somewhat true—"you wouldn't understand the Dawes, and this island, it just wouldn't make sense to you."

"Try me," I said.

Adam held still and then he breathed in a deep breath, right to the pits of his lungs. He shrugged his shoulders a little in a way that I wasn't sure whether he was working out some tension or giving some sign of indifference.

For some reason, I settled on it being the latter. "Mr Naughton," I said, being overly polite and seeming to step back into my PI shoes just for one second, "there was a woman killed this morning—*murdered.*"

This didn't seem to create any sort of stirring of emotion in Adam.

But his eyes never left my own.

"Mr Hegarty," he replied, taking me off guard slightly since I hadn't thought that he knew my surname, "What you've got to understand is that we don't *live* here, on this island—"

"What're you talking about?" I said, feeling my patience giving way just a little. "I bought a house here, I can show you the title deed if you like!"

It was then that Adam gave me a wry smile.

It must've been the first time ever that I'd seen him smile in the whole of our acquaintanceship.

And it made me furious.

But, before I could unleash my ire, he hit me with a counterpunch.

"Paper is paper, Mr Hegarty, that's all it is, but you and I know—even you who has only spent a few seasons on this island—that this land belongs to the Dawes, always has, there would never be any other way."

I thought back to my conversations with the Hubbards on the matter, about the history of the Dawes family as they had outlined it to me. But I had always taken all of that stuff with a lashing of salt. I never *really* believed that their shame was so widespread that it required an entire *island* for its dominion.

Although I knew just where Adam was headed, I didn't think to interrupt him.

"Whatever happens here," Adam continued, "whether or not people get themselves hit by cars"—he paused for a fraction of a second—"or *worse*, we, those who are *allowed* to live here, on Sinewy, should not pay it any mind. To do so would be a great folly."

For the longest time, I just kept on staring right into those inky-black eyes of his, feeling a tremble passing over the surface of my skin.

Not fear . . . or was it?

Without another word to Adam, I trudged out past him, feeling the scrub of his tattered sailor's jumper against my jacket.

6

S O OFTEN—so *many* times—the sea breeze has cooled whatever boiling emotions might be brewing inside of me. That was one of those things that led me to buy my retirement home here, on the island. The attraction of simply being able to slip out the front door, traipse down to the beach and then, gripping the metal railing, stare out into the grey sea, lose myself in the kneading waves.

Now, though—*then*—I could hardly keep myself together. It was like my whole body might burst apart out of rage. Out of the very notion of Adam's that we were merely *guests* on this island. And that we were, in some way, less than human.

Nothing more than *ants* to the Dawes family.

I wondered at what Adam meant by it being a great 'folly' for any of us to so much as *make enquiries* of Dawes Mansion . . . then again, I supposed, Marley Evermoore was the evidence which backed up the cautionary tale.

Was I better off leaving it?

The body would need explaining.

Did the Dawes' influence stretch so widely?

I gripped the metal railing tighter still. It felt ice-cold against my skin. Or, maybe, after all these years, it was my blood which had turned cold.

Back in the business I had made it my duty to go to great lengths to get the answers, to solve the puzzles, to work out whodunit.

But hadn't I already done that here?

Hadn't I drawn the killer out from between Adam Naughton's lips?

What else was there for me to achieve?

74

It wasn't like I stood to make any sort of money from 'closing' this case once and for all.

Did I really have something resembling a conscience even now, in my retirement, after I'd been taking money, all along, to debase myself with life's little miseries?

What *was* there that kept my mind from moving on?

As I turned back to my house, away from the sea, my eyes scoped the hillside, finally settled on the Dawes Mansion, standing up there, all angular, all *awkward* but somehow a constant remainder of the glory which had once reigned not just over this island but over a great amount of the country that I had left behind.

I stared at the house a long time before I noticed the attic window—before I noticed the face staring out from me there. And though I had never so much as laid an eye on her in person, only in the books which the Hubbards had shown me, the regally arranged, photographic portraits inside of those yellowing pages, I could make out her features.

For a long few heartbeats, we stared into one another's eyes, until, with an almost imperceptible flourish of curtain, Mrs Dawes disappeared, once more, into the shadows of her home.

As I trudged my way back up my front garden path, already thinking about the decanter of whisky nestled away in my drinks cabinet, I thought I could hear the *rumble* of an engine starting up. And then the *crunch* of tyres over broken-up tarmac.

I wondered if *they* would come to collect the body.

NEVER-ENDING
TREE HOUSE

Present Day

THE AIR WAS STUFFY. Too hot. At the same time it smelled of rain.

And Samantha's mouth tasted of blood.

She peered through the fogged-up window and out into the back garden of the house where she'd grown up.

The rain was pattering down, just like it always had in her mind's eye, whenever she imagined her childhood home. She observed the way that it caused the leaves on the trees to flicker as the larger drops struck, bringing into mind the reflex caused by a rubber hammer to a kneecap.

On days like these—*grey* days with the clouds all blotting out what little sunlight there was on a late-October afternoon—she couldn't help but turn her mind to the tree house, to where it jutted out, about three, four metres up in the large oak tree at the very bottom of the garden.

It was funny, pretty much as soon as Samantha—the younger sister of a pair of older brothers—had left home, the back garden had become transformed.

She still recalled her first visit back home, when she'd moved to the city, gone off to be a Big Girl, and how she'd rounded the house, checked out the garden, and found that everything was gone.

Everything that had marked it as once being a *children's* garden.

The first thing that she noted had gone was the trampoline.

But even though she felt a slight nostalgia at the thought of finding it gone, she could sympathise with her mother.

After all, she was living here now, all alone, and she didn't need a whole bunch of child's antiquities clogging up the place . . . making her feel worse about her 'empty nest.'

And the trampoline had been all sun-faded, covered in holes all over.

An 'accident waiting to happen' as her mother had often put it.

But nothing that had happened on the trampoline could compare with what had gone on in the tree house.

Samantha also noticed a whole host of other things missing from the garden.

The plastic slide, coupled with the metal climbing bars.

Gone.

The deformed ceramic gnomes they'd all cobbled together in art class—each of Samantha and her brothers attending the same school, and going through the same, well-thrashed-out, *aged* lesson plans, one year after the next.

The gnomes were gone too.

All that remained were well-pruned rose bushes, and nicely trimmed flower beds.

Everything had looked so orderly.

Never before had Samantha felt that something of herself had been swept away so readily—so easily.

And yet . . . and yet she knew that the one thing which her mother *really* would've liked to see torn down, exorcised from the garden forever more, was the tree house.

But the tree house remained.

Today it still remained.

Stuffed up there in the oak tree, in that flat section between the branches which forked on off over the garden fence, and out over the field which ran along the back of their house.

For some reason, though she couldn't quite say *why*, Samantha had been glad to see that the tree house remained.

Even though it did carry *those* memories.

She drew her gaze back from the tree house at the bottom of

their garden, moving to examine the drops of rain that rolled down the other side of the glass, right before her nose.

She could feel the chill of the rain.

Could almost feel that *chill* right down to her blood.

Could feel her heart clenching tight.

Because she knew that she was going there again . . . what another person might've called a 'trip down memory lane' . . .

Thirty Years Earlier

1

AT SIX YEARS OLD, Samantha had been terribly excited to hear the sawing of wood as she padded along the pavement, her school bag slapping against her thigh, with her brothers: Eric and Henry, on each side of her.

She could smell the sawdust on the warm summer air and it reminded her of the time when they'd gone to the zoo, and she'd breathed in the monkeys' enclosure. There had been sawdust lining the cement floor and she could remember asking her mother whether or not the monkeys liked the sawdust. When she'd got an answer, she had not been satisfied by it, but hadn't had the opportunity to follow up since one of the boy monkeys had taken that opportunity to wee up against the glass . . . much to Samantha's brothers' amusement.

That day, on the walk home from school, she had been sucking on a toffee that Henry had slipped her. Though she knew that her mother *didn't think* that she understood everything she talked about with other mums, Samantha well knew, from overheard conversations, that Henry—her oldest brother—would be leaving their school next year to go to a bigger, *more-grown-up* one. And so, for that reason, she'd sort of got into a silly habit of telling herself to cherish every last moment she had with him.

Because soon he would be gone.

Henry had the responsibility of bringing her and Eric back from their school, and Samantha knew that it was a Very Important Job, and one which Henry took extremely seriously.

The rules were clear.

Henry would not permit dawdling.

He would not permit laughing, or giggling of any sort.

And he insisted that, at *all* times, both Samantha and Eric hold tightly to his hand as they navigated the five-minute walk from the school.

Today, though, it was different.

And Samantha *forgot* the rules.

Though they were only a couple of houses from arriving back home, the rules were clear. That Samantha was to keep hold of Henry's hand till they could feel the *crunch* of the gravel drive beneath the hard treads of their school shoes.

But Samantha didn't wait.

That sound of sawing.

That *smell* of sawdust floating on the air.

She simply *had* to go after it.

Had to investigate.

And so, like a naughty puppy, she took Henry by surprise and peeled her fingers away from his.

Just like that, she was off and running.

Paying no attention at all to Henry and Eric calling her back.

As she sprinted on around the side of the house, the gravel pinging up against the bare backs of her legs, to that spot where her school skirt didn't cover, the sound of sawing got louder. The smell of the sawdust was so thick in the air that Samantha was almost certain that if she was to take a chomp of the air, right then and there, she would come away with sawdust in her mouth.

But she had no time to go chomping on air.

She had investigating to do.

As she brought the verdant garden into view, she caught sight of the man standing at the back there, sawing away at planks of wood.

She saw that he already had a whole stack of sawn-up wood beside him.

As she brought him into focus, took in his sun-faded overalls that might once have been black, but which were now more of a greyish purple, she felt that familiar skittering feeling, down in her stomach. The way that her confidence seemed to suddenly leave her just as soon as she came across a stranger—and especially somebody who her mother hadn't sanctioned.

But she already stood on the concrete slabs of the patio which ran across the back of their house, and before she could think to act, the stranger raised his head.

Smiled at her.

He held his saw down at his thigh and said, "Well, hello there!"

Samantha felt trapped. Over her shoulder, she could hear the familiar *crunch* of gravel. Her brothers arriving. She hoped to herself that they would follow her around the side of the house, rather than knock on the front door.

". . . Hello," Samantha got out finally.

The man had a stubbly, black beard, and he wore a pair of dungarees that looked baggy on him. He wore a white t-shirt underneath that was covered in all sorts of muck and grease and sweat. "You've grown since I last saw you," he said.

Samantha cocked her head to one side. She didn't quite know what to make of him. She thought about what her mother said about strangers, and that she was never to trust them. She knew that the thing to do was for her to go inside, or maybe to knock on the sliding patio doors, and to go fetch her mother.

But wasn't this different?

The man *was* in their back garden after all.

And he was sawing wood.

How would he have got here if it hadn't been for her mother giving him permission?

Samantha held still, and she felt the presence of her brothers arrive behind her.

The man shifted his glance over her head and onto them.

"Would you look at that," he said, "the whole gang's in town now."

Something about the man Samantha didn't like at all, though she really couldn't put her finger on it. She just felt uncomfortable with him there. Like he might be *scary* . . . or something.

Thankfully, a few moments later, her mother did slide back the doors to the garden, and Samantha took the opportunity to rush at her, just like she always did when she finished school. Her mother asked the man with the saw whether he would like some tea and then she went inside to make it.

When Samantha asked her mother about the man, about what it was he was doing, she told her that he was building a tree house. A tree house for Samantha and her brothers to play in.

Samantha still didn't feel right about it.

2

THAT NIGHT, Samantha knelt up on her bed and she peeled back the blinds to look on out into the back garden. She had always liked the way that her bedroom faced into the back garden. It was like she had a peephole on a secret kingdom.

All the other rooms in the house either faced towards their neighbours' houses at either side or, in the case of her mother's, they faced the busy main road.

In the late-summer sunshine, the sun still lighting everything up, she made out the man there manoeuvring the planks of wood into position in the oak tree. Onto that flat-bottomed section a few metres up from the ground.

He had a pencil stuck behind his ear and as he worked he jabbed his tongue out of the corner of his mouth. Once, when he glanced back over his shoulder, looked back in the direction of the house, Samantha had to duck down.

When she looked up again—looked back out into the garden —the man had gone.

She guessed that he had gone home.

Or that he had come inside *their* home.

3

T HE NEXT DAY, after school, Samantha gripped Henry's hand tighter and tighter as they got close to their house. Today she couldn't hear sawing, but she did hear hammering.

And she didn't like it.

She wanted that sound to stop.

It sent skitters across the surface of her skin to hear it.

But, as she well knew, being the youngest in the house, she had little to no power at making demands about *anything*.

As they crunched on into the gravel driveway, her brothers dragged her on in the direction of the back garden.

But Samantha didn't *want* to go that way.

So she tugged them towards the front door.

"Come on!" Henry said, those wrinkles of exertion digging into his face—those wrinkles which Samantha always saw on his face when he was working hard on his homework.

Both Henry and Eric worked together, continued to drag her on in the direction of the back garden.

And Samantha was powerless to stop them.

She breathed in the sawdust today, but it smelled a little fainter, like it had been dulled just a touch by the summer breeze, and the scent of flowers and freshly cut grass had returned to wipe it away somewhat.

As they rounded the side of the house, sure enough, the man was there again, a hammer in his hand as he worked on nailing the planks into the tree.

Today he had a ladder, and he stood perched on the top, working at the oak tree, nailing on the planks into that little recess in the centre of it.

Something about the image just looked bad to Samantha.

She couldn't decide whether she didn't want the man there, or the *tree house*.

Maybe it was both.

The man smiled widely at the boys, and he allowed them to take turns with the hammer, for them to nail the planks onto the tree.

When Samantha sensed she could get away with it, she slipped away from the boys, and returned inside, to see her mother.

Where she felt safe.

4

ANOTHER FEW DAYS LATER—maybe it was more than a week—Samantha returned home from school to find the tree house finished. All up there, in the middle of the oak tree.

As she stood on the patio, she couldn't help but take in the slanted roof, the way that the pale grey wood stood proud, and *angular*. She looked to the little rope ladder which led up to the opening in the side.

Her brothers, of course, rushed off straightaway.

Samantha looked around first, saw that there was no sign of the man, and then she headed on after her brothers. Feeling a little more apprehensive about the whole thing.

As her brothers followed one another up the rope ladder, and headed on to explore the tree house, Samantha stood several metres away from them, not wanting to encroach on their fun. It didn't seem like there was enough space up there for more than two anyway.

"Cross?" came the voice.

The *man's* voice.

Samantha turned. Saw that he had emerged from the back doors of the house. And that he was smiling. Just like always.

As he approached her, he mimicked her pout, and crossed his arms over his chest.

Then, apparently unable to contain himself, he broke out into a chuckle. When he got closer to her still, he reached forwards and ruffled her hair.

His touch sent a shudder down her spine.

"Look just like your mother when you're cross," he said, and then, crouching down to her level, "Not the adventurous type, huh?"

Samantha wouldn't have been able to say anything if she'd wanted to.

The man frightened her.

He seemed to cause the words to dissolve in her mouth.

"Well," the man said, straightening back up, and then dipping one hand in the stomach pocket of his dungarees, "How about I help you up there, huh?"

Samantha felt a prickle inside her veins, like her blood had turned to ice suddenly, and now it was thawing just as quickly.

When he reached out to take hold of her, to lift her from underneath her arms, she didn't resist. She just surrendered herself to his hold.

As he lugged her over to the tree house, to where her brothers were already having a finger-gun war, ducking and diving out from the wooden structure, she breathed in the thick, sour smell of the man's sweat. The cologne that he wore, and which reminded her of some woody herb she didn't know the name of.

When they got to the tree house, he lifted her up high, and she stuck out her feet to land on the wooden planks of the entrance.

"You got a hold?" the man said.

Samantha grabbed onto the side of the tree house and then felt Henry's sure hand take hold of her forearm, and help her in.

"I've got her!" Henry said.

And, with that command, the man released her.

Gave her over to Henry.

Inside, the tree house smelled strongly of the man's sweat, and wood, of course.

There was a window in the back which looked out over the field which ran along the back of the house, and in the distance she could make out the sparkle of the sun off the windows of the nearby city.

The floor wasn't completely flat, and she guessed that was

because, where the tree house rested, on top of this oak tree, it wasn't level either.

As she stood up there, looking on out over the fields, she wondered if she'd been wrong about the tree house. If she—*really*—hadn't understood it.

Sometimes she didn't understand things.

"Let's have a look!" Eric said, elbowing her out of the way.

Henry chided him a little, but he took up the position which Eric had freed Samantha from just the same.

With nothing else much to do, Samantha headed on towards the opening of the tree house. She looked down at the grass, seemingly *such* a long way away.

The man wasn't there any longer, and when she looked up, she realised that he was now standing over at the patio, with her mother.

Her mother was wearing a peach-coloured summer dress which clung to her figure with the summer breeze. It was strange. Samantha could hardly remember *ever* seeing her mother wearing a dress, and, even then, at six years old, she wondered if her mother was wearing one that day because of the man.

Right as Samantha was about to call out to them, to ask the man to come and get her down, she watched the man, holding a perspiring glass of lemonade her mother had brought out, arc his neck towards her mother.

And they kissed.

Samantha felt a ticklish feeling in her gut. Almost apart from herself, she bunched her fingers into fists. Eyed up the grass beneath her.

And leaped off.

5

SAMANTHA'S MOTHER banned them from playing on the tree house.

Nobody was allowed to play on the tree house in case they had an accident.

And so, for the rest of the summer, nobody did, though Samantha caught Eric, and his friends, bobbing about it on a few occasions.

All that Samantha had to do to put them off clambering up the rope ladder was to slink on out onto the patio with one of her dolls, showing off the pink cast on her broken arm. That was enough for Eric to call his friends away from the tree house, and they'd usually jump the fence and head into the fields that ran along the back of the house.

All things considered, Samantha was fairly glad with the development.

The man had gone away, apparently never to return, and life showed signs of returning to normality.

As the years cranked by, and Samantha and her brothers got older, the tree house stood neglected. Weeds and moss grew all over it. The rain stained it a dirty grey colour. And, whenever Samantha found herself down there, at the bottom of the garden, she noted how there were now several rotten holes in the wooden planks where the weather had got in.

Some days, as she looked out of her bedroom window upon waking up, and down into the garden, she almost managed to convince herself that the tree house was gone.

That, one day—quite simply—she'd wake to find that she'd imagined the whole episode.

But the tree house never went away.

It was *always* there.

Waiting for her whenever she got back from school.

But it wasn't till Samantha turned eleven and headed to the same school her brothers had gone to that she thought of it as anything other than an eyesore.

As something which seemed to strain against the otherwise beautiful—*natural*—oak tree at the bottom of the garden.

It was coming into October when it happened.

Samantha knew because she'd been at school just long enough to begin to let go of the friends who had followed her from her previous school and to embrace the new ones.

And she could see her breath forming before her in the air as she plodded on home, rucksack sagging down at her back, away from the bus stop.

Her brothers were walking ahead of her, of course.

Eric and Henry, fourteen and sixteen, respectively, and a group of friends hung about them like a swarm of flies.

Though Samantha had been at their school for a short time, she had learned that both of her brothers were in with the *sporty* crowd. And, sure enough, all their friends were skinny as bean-poles with the first buds of biceps, the scrawny flesh over their stomachs in the process of hardening into a solid *muscular* abdomen.

And one of them always—*always*—seemed to be tossing, or kicking a ball about between the group. Today it was a cricket ball. Bright red. Shining a little dully in the early-October evening, and Samantha wondered what they were doing with a cricket ball considering that the season had been over for a good month or more.

Perhaps she should have seen what would happen then.

But, for whatever reason, she didn't.

She couldn't quite stomach her brothers' friends and so she skulked on up to her bedroom, spread her homework out on her desk, and blinked on the desk lamp to get started.

For Samantha, homework was something of a novelty still . . . and one which hadn't yet worn off for her . . . though she heard all about school how everybody was *supposed* to hate homework, she found it quite soothing, in a way.

How she'd turn a clean page in her exercise book, mark out the current date in the blue ink from her fountain pen. How she'd blow the ink dry so that she didn't smudge it with her fist as she wrote out the title.

And then, in her neat, looping, handwriting, she would begin.

Scrawling down maths equations.

Marking out methods and conclusions from science experiments.

Etching out a paragraph of analysis for an English assignment.

She didn't care *what* subject it was, she just enjoyed the act, the act of watching her writing appear on the page.

She must've been going at her homework all of five minutes when, outside, she heard a low *thud*. She straightened up in her chair, glanced about herself, as if it might be coming from her own bedroom and then, not hearing anything further, she got her nose back down in her exercise and continued.

Thud.

Thud.

Thud-thud-thud!

Then there was a quake of laughter.

That deep-throated, uncontrolled tone of the boys in Henry's year at school.

It was funny to think about it, about how those boys hadn't seemed to have grown into their voices yet. To see them standing there, all gawky and spotty, and then to hear their *men's* voices.

Samantha knew the signs of trouble when she heard them and she kept her nose down in her exercise book, not wanting to get herself wrapped up in whatever it was her brothers were playing at. Already she'd found herself being the object of games —of practical 'jokes.'

Almost all of the jokes involved the boys using her makeup, or trying on one of her bras, or stealing her mobile phone . . . and every joke was just as tiresome as the last.

Thud. Thud. Thud.

The noise went on for another minute or so before Samantha realised she couldn't take it any longer. She slapped her fountain pen down on the centrefold of her exercise book and pranced on over to the window.

From where she stood, she looked on out there, out at the boys all gathered around the tree house at the bottom of the garden.

Though the light was fading, she could just about make them out there.

She watched on, doing her best not to show too much of her face in the window—lest they decide they were bored with that game and come along to bother her   and she saw Eric reel back his arm and then toss the cricket ball hard at the side of the tree house.

Thunk!

She thought she could hear a light splinter of the wood too, the ball making to break through.

She was certain that she should've felt glad about what they were doing, about how the boys were all, apparently, working on destroying the tree house.

And yet, something deep inside of herself, it wouldn't *allow* her to simply stand up there and do nothing at all.

It was only when she saw the first puff of smoke—one of the boys in the group blowing out cigarette smoke—that she thought to move.

Their mother only enforced a few rules about the house, and she hardly had the energy to enforce *those*, and one of them was that none of them—*ever*—under any circumstances, was to bring cigarettes into the house.

Alcohol was a little more negotiable.

But still strictly controlled.

And, of course, the tree house was *strictly* out of bounds.

When her mother wasn't home, Samantha saw herself as a kind of de-facto guardian of the sanctity of their home, the one who was responsible for keeping her brothers in line despite them being three and five years older than her respectively.

She trotted down the stairs, stormed on through the kitchen, and then out through the patio doors.

Once out there, she saw the puffs of smoke more distinctly.

When she breathed in, she became aware that the smoke didn't have the usual cigarette odour to it. No, it had something of a sweeter note. And though she really couldn't have said as much out loud, she wondered, years later, if she'd known all along what it was.

Her focus soon moved on, however, to Henry, who was climbing up the rope ladder, heading upwards into the tree house.

She felt her gut clench tight, and she wanted to call out for him to get down from there.

But her throat dried up.

There were lots of boys there, at the bottom of the garden, lots of Eric and Henry's friends, and she knew that if she so much as made a *peep* they would most likely jump her . . . maybe force her up into the tree house and keep her there prisoner till their mother came home.

And so she found herself relegated to a simple spectator.

She watched Henry—grinning all over—clamber his way on up into the tree house. And then disappear inside of it.

While he was gone, Samantha took in all the dents the boys had made with the cricket ball so far. She could even see a few splinters lying about in the long grass, the pieces that had fallen down.

She felt her heart beating hard against her ribs, and she would've done anything to stop it . . . to stop whatever it was that was happening right at that moment.

But, at the same time, she felt powerless.

A victim of circumstance.

It was only when she eyed Henry emerging, grinning from ear to ear, the cricket ball clutched in his fist, that she *really* felt that burning feeling pass through her blood.

His eyes, slowly, settled onto hers.

She watched those frown lines appear in his forehead, like they always did when he was concentrating hard on some problem or other.

His lips parted slightly when he lost his balance.

And a full-blooded scream leaped out from his lungs as he fell.

Samantha watched on in horror as Henry tumbled down from the tree house, his head striking several branches on the way.

And when he hit the grass he lay still.

Totally still.

And everything was silent.

Just for a couple of moments.

And then there was bedlam.

S AMANTHA drew herself away from the window, broke her gaze set on the tree house, still sitting up there in the tree after all these years. Almost as if mimicking the raindrops sliding down the outside of the window, she felt a tear sneak out from her eye, and roll down her cheek.

"Samantha?"

Samantha wiped her teardrop off her cheek before she turned around. Before she took in her mother, standing there, a tray bearing a pair of cups of tea and a plate with a trio of buttered scones.

Samantha had always wondered why her mother liked to pick odd numbers—why if there were two of them she always went off to fetch *three* biscuits, or *three* pieces of fruit. It was almost as if her mother wanted to be the one to give the extra snack up . . . the one to be *polite*.

Her mother set the tray down on the glass coffee table which sat between the pair of armchairs in the sitting room.

On impulse, as Samantha always found whenever she stood in the sitting room, her eyes settled on the photograph on the mantelpiece. The photograph of her and her two brothers—Eric and Henry. It had been taken on a sunny afternoon, that same summer when Henry had tumbled out of the tree house and broken his neck . . . been 'taken from them' as her mother liked to put it.

From their smiles, from the way the sun beamed over their faces, almost seeming to set them each in a saintly glow, Samantha could hardly believe the tragedy that waited just around the corner for them all.

That would change their lives forever.

"Milk?" her mother said, clutching the dainty, white porcelain decanter.

Samantha smiled. "Just a little."

Her mother poured it out.

"Thanks," Samantha said, thinking about how her mother knew *exactly* how she took her tea, that she'd had thirty-six years in which to work out how she took her tea.

And yet she still asked . . .

Her mother sat down in one of the armchairs, but Samantha remained standing at the window which looked out at the back garden as if to move away might break something intrinsic within herself.

As if it might be an acknowledgement of defeat.

But *what* defeat?

"The tree house," Samantha said, looking out the window again. "I know why you never had it taken down."

"Hmm?" her mother said, in that way of hers that made it seem that she either hadn't heard . . . or hadn't *comprehended* exactly what Samantha had just said.

That reaction really got on her nerves.

But Samantha pushed those thoughts from her mind for the time being.

"It reminded you of him, didn't it?" Samantha said.

"Of who, darling?" her mother said, taking a sip from her steaming cup of tea.

Samantha felt the lump form in her throat. She swallowed it down. She forced herself to look away from the tree house, to look back at her mother, seated in her armchair. "Of our father."

Her mother stayed still for a long time. She didn't move a muscle. Though this had been a long-understood truth in the whole family . . . which was to say between herself, Eric and her mother . . . it was also an unspoken one.

Either something which was so obvious as to not require explanation, or something so painful as to be torture to discuss openly.

Perhaps her mother had thought that she'd been naïve, that at only six years old Samantha never would've understood the *true nature* of her mother's relationship with the man in the dungarees.

But she was wrong.

"Why did he do it?" Samantha said. "The tree house, I mean?"

Her mother seemed to drift off into a daze, her focus sought out some position in mid-air which could only mean she was scuttling about in her cabinet of memories, of her personal history so deeply repressed.

When her mother spoke, her tone was so soft, so brittle that Samantha was afraid that she might be about to faint. "He wanted something . . . something for you to remember him by."

Samantha sniffed, looked to her mug of tea on the coffee table, still steaming away. "Wouldn't it have been better if he'd been around—if he'd been there . . . *with us* . . . *his children?*"

Her mother blinked away her daze. Seemed to bring the world back into focus. And then, gradually, she craned her neck upwards to meet Samantha's eye. "He was sick, your father, he . . . didn't have long left." She paused, drew in a deep breath, then added, "He wanted to come along and say goodbye, he was enough of a man to do that."

Samantha held her mother's gaze for a few seconds and then, as if something within her snapped, she broke it off and looked on out through the window. Out into the garden. To the tree house. And she watched Henry's fall play out in her mind again —just as it had in her nightmares ever since that day.

Always tumbling.

Falling down.

And always—*always without exception*—that never-ending tree house looming above.

LEADEN FINGERS
TWISTED

W HENEVER I LOOK DOWN into the River Gour, I
can't help but see the muck at the bottom.
It's just a habit I've acquired.

And I openly admit it's not particularly *ladylike*.

Though the Environmental Authorities around here have
spent good time—*even better money*—on trying to fish out every last
plastic, six-pack ring, to get shot of all of the decaying nappies,
not to mention the bulbous, yellowing, used condoms; all that I've
noticed is, at best, a slowing in the decay of human civilisation.

And they've been able to do the square root of *fuck all* about
the stench.

. . . The *stench* . . . God Almighty, the river stinks of fish heads
and boiled petrol and raw sewage. Enough to bring the bitter
taste of bile to the back of my throat.

I might've been able to stand even those things if it hadn't
been for the accompanying soundtrack.

Or, to put it more accurately, the *deafening* silence.

I never truly *knew* the meaning of that phrase till I happened
upon the Gour.

But, as I stood there, on the slippery, slightly green, muddy
bank of the Gour, I realised that I couldn't hear any bird calls—
to be expected—but that I couldn't even hear so much as an old
faithful trawler engine puttering into life.

It seemed almost as if humans had abandoned this sad little
stretch.

Perhaps I should've taken their lead.

But I was there on business.

God *knows* nothing else would've brought me there.

Auburn Spector, Private Investigator.

As I felt a cool, October breeze whip its way along the water, arriving from out at sea, I suppose, I reached up and did up the top three toggles of my duffel coat. I produced a pair of brown leather gloves from within the pockets of my coat and slipped them over my grateful, gooseflesh-stricken hands. The fuzzy material inside kept my skin cosy. Sent a slight warmth through my blood. And, all wrapped up like that, I felt like I could just about think again without having to suffer through constant shuddering.

As I stood up on the bank, I promised myself that—when I got home—I'd take a look at a quick holiday to somewhere sunny, somewhere the thermometer had the nerve to creep up and over ten degrees Celsius.

But business first.

I glanced back over my shoulder, getting that unnerving feeling that somebody might be watching. But, just as always with my paranoid urges, there was nobody there at all. I could see the roof of my midnight-blue, third-hand hatchback peeping just up above the cement wall—tipped with barbed wire—which ran about the periphery of the banks of the River Gour.

All alone.

Just how I liked it.

At least where *work* was involved . . .

I traced the surface of the grey, lifeless water, trying to see something—*anything*—that might give me some kind of a clue to the current case. I recalled the meeting, earlier that afternoon, the shaken-up young guy—perhaps just about into his twenties— with blond hair and wearing a pair of oiled-up overalls.

A car mechanic, I had thought, but he'd soon set me right.

Told me that he was a welder.

For the first few moments of our conversation, I'd been so struck by the fragile, birdlike cheekbones, and the wispy bit of blond fluff above his lip, that I'd been unable to concentrate on his words.

Sometimes you get a lot by looking at a person.

And sometimes *not*.

Because—to all manner of appearance—the boy didn't seem to have anything approaching the money to pay for my private-investigation services.

The brown envelope—a thousand quid nestled inside—soon swung me around.

A good month's expenses.

Up front.

And more to come if I could see the case through.

When the boy'd left, I'd gone to go see Tony—one of my underworld associates, and an expert forger—who assured me that each and every one of the twenty-pound notes which made up the thousand pounds was legit.

That sent my mind spinning some more.

I admit to wondering if it was a setup.

Some sort of a joke.

But I couldn't think of who might play such a joke.

And where was the punchline?

The boy—the car mechanic called 'Paul'—told me that he was looking for a girl. About his age. Perhaps a couple of years younger, since I hadn't thought to ask for my client's age.

I guess I still have some semblance of manners intact.

Paul told me that Ginger—as he referred to her—had gone missing about a month ago. And that he'd been unable to get in touch with her by her mobile. That she wasn't home from what he could decipher . . . when I pushed him for what this might mean, I got the impression that he'd rung the doorbell to her flat several times, and got no response.

For whatever reason, he didn't want to contact the police.

When I asked him, strictly for professional reasons, whether this 'Ginger' might be his girlfriend, his cheeks coloured. He became evasive. And I—politely—chose to drop the subject.

He seemed glad for that.

As Paul had got up from the battered old wooden chair opposite my desk—the sort of chair that I imagined, in a previous life, had probably belonged in some community centre—he suggested that I come out to the River Gour. That he'd heard chatter about his workshop which suggested I might find some clue to Ginger's disappearance down there.

He wouldn't elaborate further.

He had only withdrawn a torn-off section of map; a toddler-like, red-pencilled ring drawn about a particular spot. And I had to force myself not to smile.

So, there I was, an hour later, a thousand pounds richer, standing on the bank of the River Gour.

Freezing my tits off.

2

I 'D LIKE TO SAY that it became quickly obvious just why
Paul had sent me down to that *very specific* spot on the bank of
the River Gour . . . and I'd like to say that, when I returned to
my hatchback, tuned into the radio and listened to the lottery
numbers, that I turned millionairess.

But I didn't.

Some things just aren't meant to be.

I sat there, behind the wheel, the engine trundling, and
welcome streams of hot air pumping out through the vents.

Giving that strange, slightly artificial sense of warmth which
car heaters seem to give.

Either the first, or second, owner of the hatchback had been
a smoker. I hadn't previously considered this factor. Never *really*
understood all the fuss about whether goods—*items*—had come
from a 'smoke-free' home or not.

But I understood it now.

As I sat there, in the car, I could almost *feel* the cigarette
smoke oozing out of the upholstery, in brown, cartoonish waves.
Tickling my nostrils. Making me want to sneeze. I can recall—
more than one occasion—when I was doing some pretty good
speed on the motorway only to find my sinuses tingling and
having to pull over to get a few sneezes out.

I tried everything suggested.

From professional cleaning—most expensive—to leaving a
bowl of coffee grains in the footwell of the passenger seat for a
fortnight.

No dice.

The stink of smoke remains.

And I found myself actually *speculating* as to whether I should
maybe take up smoking—take *some kind* of activity up to stave off

109

my loneliness—when I observed, over the top of the wheel, on the other side of my half-condensed windscreen, a pair of men trudging along gently on the bank of the river.

It was so strange.

I almost felt like I had been sleeping while the world ended.

Like I'd happened to be standing on the bank of the River Gour when some Russians, or Chinese, or the Americans—the British?—had decided to belatedly drop the nuke.

And perhaps it so happened that that particular section of the River Gour was so entirely toxic already that such an attack had had little effect.

One of the men wore a denim jacket; the other had on a leather coat which swept just below his kneecaps. Both men had their heads tilted down. Staring at their toes. Hands stuffed into their pockets. It was a strange sight because if I'd seen either man in isolation, one or the other of them trudging along the street with that pose—even along the deserted river bank here—I would've thought nothing at all of it.

What made it strange was that these men were *clearly* in one another's company.

And I caught that sensation which gets me thinking about the can of pepper spray I keep locked up in the glove compartment.

It's been a sticky road, but, over time, I've learned to *listen* to that sensation.

As I leaned over the passenger seat, clicked the glove compartment open, I heard a twin tap of knuckles against the driver's window.

It sent a chill up my spine.

I almost jumped right up and smashed my head on the car roof.

In the fading daylight, with my glove compartment opened and the small, cloth pouch containing the pepper spray exposed, I glanced over my shoulder.

To the window.

Saw that there was a silhouette.

Nothing more than a dark shape.

Now, back when I was young and idealistic—*wanting to be a team player*—I might've failed every exam for police going, but that didn't mean I didn't have some common sense. And, right then, common sense informed me, rather strongly *urged* me, that opening up my door here, on the bank of the River Gour to some strange, decidedly *shady* figure was not anywhere near being a good idea.

So, instead, I wound down the window.

Just a crack.

Enough so that I would be able to hear what this person had to say.

I soon established that it was a female security guard. That she wore one of those—*deeply institutional*—grey-blue uniforms. She had a night stick down at her side, and I vaguely pondered about the legality of such a thing . . . but didn't quite feel like taking the matter up with her right there and then.

She had gelled, smoothed-down black hair—pinned into a bun around the back of her head—and a pair of striking eyebrows.

The same shade of black as her hair.

She held her lips pert, tightly shut for a couple of seconds before saying, "Can't park here, this's private property."

I smiled back as pleasantly as I could manage and then put on my best bimbo voice as I replied, "Oh, I hadn't realised."

The security guard straightened up, glanced around and then said, "You're lucky it's just me here—if my boss was about he'd stick you with a fine."

"Would he?" I replied, again sounding a little bimbo-like.

"Most likely."

With the security guard fixing me with a watchful glare, I

reversed out of the space where I had parked up the hatchback, simultaneously snapping shut the glove compartment.

But not without first slipping the pepper spray, snug and safe, into my coat pocket.

The road out of the car park led away from the banks of the River Gour, and I soon found myself trundling along Industrial Estate Hell, all five-miles-per-hour signs and corrugated-steel rooftops. I looked for a turning that would lead me back to the bank of the river, but I really had no luck at all.

When I reached a dead end, I pulled a pretty successful U-turn—*for me*—and drove back along the way I had come.

It was when I got to the—now closed-off—parking spaces where I'd left the hatchback, that I caught the eye of the security guard. She now sat inside a brightly lit booth beside the entrance to the lot, and I could see that she had a magazine spread out before her on some desk, or alcove, or whatever those tiny, shelf-like constructions within guard booths are called.

She glanced up casually to me.

Her eyes met mine.

I left the engine idling.

Thought things over.

Guessed it was worth a shot.

I bucked the car up onto the curb and switched off the engine.

Stepped out into the brutal, gritty weather moving over the industrial estate.

3

NOW THAT I was no longer parked up on the private property the security guard was patrolling, she seemed far more receptive of me. As I stood in the doorway to the booth, she even deigned to give me a gentle smile. "Not got yourself lost, have you?"

As I peered about the inside of the guard booth, I spotted a conked-out portable TV—one of those with a screen about the size of a matchbox—and I absorbed the odd smell of machine grease and body odour emanating from within.

I supposed that those scents were sourced from the security guard's daytime colleagues.

Males.

A tiny electric heater buzzed away at the security guard's feet, and I felt its waves of warmth up against my cheeks.

Most welcoming.

I saw, off at the security guard's elbow, that there was a see-through, plastic box containing a still-wrapped sandwich, a bag of crisps and a chocolate bar.

I guessed that it was her dinner.

It certainly sent a few hunger pangs rattling through my belly.

My gaze finally swept back onto the security guard's. "I was just wondering," I said, "if you might've seen anything odd about here." I hooked my thumb in the direction of the banks of the River Gour. "You know, I saw those two men walking along the water. You wouldn't know anything about them would you?"

The security guard snorted up some phlegm.

Then she swallowed it down.

She twitched her nose a few times, then shook her head and said, "I stick to my patch—which means all the way to that barbed-wire fence, up to this booth here." As she spoke, she indicated exactly where she meant with brash flurries of her arms. Then she turned her attention downwards once more, back to her magazine. "That's all I get paid for."

Now, I might not be the zenith of private eye-dom, but I can certainly spot somebody crying out for a bribe.

Making a mental note to add it to my notebook of expenses in my glove compartment later, I reached into my purse, removed five clean, crisp twenty-pound notes, and laid them down before the security guard in a fan.

Right on top of her magazine.

The security guard twitched her nose another couple of times.

She coughed.

Then she laid her hand—ever so gently—over the top of the money.

She craned her neck back to me. And then glanced upwards, to the corner of the booth, where I now realised hung a surveillance camera.

Its bright-red light shining away.

It pointed back towards the river.

She gave me a broad smile, outstretching her other hand for a shake, then said, "Name's Gemma, you want the full tour, or what?"

4

AFTER 'GEMMA' had done *something* with the camera—unplugged it?—she led me over the sad, cracked-up cement car park, with its faded-away white markings indicating each of the parking bays. Then she took me down the staircase which led to the bank of the River Gour.

Together, we walked along the squidgy, green mud almost like a pair of lesbian lovers taking in a marvellous sunset.

I guess it *could've* been termed a sunset.

That was to say that, among all that grey, mottled-together cloud, I could just about make out a patch which was just a touch brighter than the rest.

. . . It could *easily* have been the sun.

The stink of fish seemed to have got worse, as the breeze coming off the water had dialled itself down a few notches. And the stench of sewage hung in the air, almost as if it was designed to send me scurrying for one of the tissues I kept in a packet in my pocket.

We were walking in the opposite direction to where the men had headed.

Going back the way they had come.

I speculated that, if it hadn't been for the interruption, I would've gone along that way all by myself . . . if I had found another way back down to the river I surely would've done.

But there I was now—my purse a hundred pounds lighter.

Gemma took the lead, and she produced a hefty torch from her utility belt, and promptly set about shining a mangy, yellow circle of light onto the river bank ahead.

We passed beneath a bridge, which I can only describe as 'piss-stinking,' and out the other side . . . to where the River Gour really looked just as it had before.

It was then that I was glad to have Gemma for company because I might've missed the large warehouse she pointed out to our left.

A little way up the river bank.

She dropped her voice to a whisper, as if she expected to be overheard. "Hardly ever see anybody along this stretch. Not walking across this shit."

She was referring to the bank of—what could *only* be described in polite terms as—'sewage-strewn muck.'

"First time I saw them," Gemma went on, "I thought they was half mad. Actually, first time that I saw them down there, I was patrolling up near the wall. Called down, asked them what they was doing." She shook her head and smiled slightly. "Ain't never seen a pair of guys so spooked in all their lives. Thought they'd gone and shit their pants. Clearly they was up to some-thing—that they didn't want anybody to see what they was up to."

I turned my attention back to the warehouse which loomed above us now. And then to the rusted-up gate with several chains and sturdy-looking padlocks wrapped about it. "And what is it that they're up to?"

Gemma just tapped her nose and trod on.

5

E VERY TIME I remind myself that I'm a real-life, breathing and bleeding, private dick, I half blind myself in wonder about how few skills I've acquired.

And one of those which has always eluded me is the fine art of lock-picking.

I can't quite think to count how many times I've wanted this or that lock opened, and been unable to find a way.

Well, all I can say is that I was getting full value for my bribe.

Gemma produced what looked like a set of keys from her belt and set to work on the padlocks. Twenty seconds flat, and she had all three—or were there *four?*—of the padlocks undone, and hanging off their chains.

As she snapped the rusted-up shackles open, she said, in a slightly smug way, "Misspent youth, and all that."

"Yeah," I said, with a wry smile back, stepping through the now-open gate, "comes in handy, though?"

She just shrugged. "Used to have a saying about it, 'leaden fingers twisted.' "

I took in the warehouse which stood before us, and the alley which ran along the side. Up ahead, I could see that there was a door with a fluorescent, orange bulb flickering away above it. Almost as if somebody had taken pains to mark out the way into the building. "And what does it mean?" I said, referring to the phrase Gemma had just spouted.

"Just about the action of opening up the padlock—nothing fancy."

"Right," I said, treading along the cracked-up concrete path, and towards the orange, flickering light, "sayings are what make the rich tapestry of our culture, huh?"

"Uh huh," Gemma said, following on my heels, "guess you could put it that way."

6

G EMMA, too, made light work of the side door to the warehouse. Although I didn't think to ask—Rule One of working with an accomplice is never to spook them: intentionally, or otherwise—I guessed from the context that there wouldn't be anybody about the warehouse at this time.

When we emerged into the warehouse, I immediately breathed in the dusty-looking air.

And, right after, coughed it back out again.

"Got allergies?" Gemma said, casually.

I managed a controlled sneeze into a tissue, then replied, "Yeah, you could say that."

Gemma led us along the wall of the warehouse, past sack upon sack of . . . what?

"Wheat," Gemma said, without my prompting, "they get it all in here and then ship it further into the city, for processing."

"Right," I replied, looking down at the endless, silhouetted rows of sacks with a dawning understanding.

"Office is up there," Gemma said, flashing her torch off in the direction of a steel staircase, at the top of which was a boxy office with interior windows.

"I take it you've been here before?" I said.

Even in the half light of her torch, I could see that Gemma was grinning. "Can't blame a girl for getting bored, can you? When I saw the way those two reacted to me, I knew that I *had* to come have a look over the place."

Feeling like the frost which'd settled over our early acquaintance had pretty much thawed, I decided to ask, "You haven't happened to see a girl around here at all?"

I thought of the photograph which Paul had given me, tucked neatly inside the pocket of my jacket, beside the can of pepper spray. I reached in and then brought it out. I held it up to Gemma so that she might shine her torchlight on it.

Gemma screwed up her features, sending shadows dancing playfully all across her tight, unwrinkled face. She stared at the picture for a good ten seconds or more before she handed it back to me with a shake of her head. "Nah," she said, "ain't seen nobody like that around here."

There was something in Gemma's demeanour—the way that she seemed to *refuse* to meet my eye which told me that she knew more than she was letting on.

I decided to leave the matter alone.

For now.

"Listen," Gemma said, "you take my torch, yeah? And I'll meet you outside when you're done, okay?"

"You're not coming up to the office?"

She shook her head. "Nah, I'll wait outside."

There was certainly some kind of an unquietness about Gemma now—as if she had just realised how much trouble she'd landed herself in.

I wondered if there might be something I could say so that she'd regain her trust in me, but, in the end, I decided to leave it.

"What if the office is locked?" I said.

Gemma gave me a smile as she handed the torch over. "It's not—don't worry."

"Okay," I said, taking the heavy torch from her, and then, after shining its light on her, watching as she retreated for the door out of the warehouse, I turned my attention to the office above.

To the staircase.

To the answers which might await me.

7

THE OFFICE SMELLED of old farts and musky body odour and—worst of all—like somebody had tried to cover said smells with a good few cans of deodorant.

I whipped out a fresh tissue to cover my mouth and nose, and navigated the half dozen, stained mugs of tea which sat on the desk—teabags stuck to their bottoms and some, I was sure, even with the handicap of the poor light from the torch, growing mould.

There was a reclining desk chair. One of those ones with the wheels taken off its base so it won't move about on a slick-surfaced floor. It sat—I estimated—about a metre away from the desk, pretty much the perfect distance for some slacker to put his feet up.

Or to make himself comfortable to speak on the phone.

There was a pair of stainless-steel filing cabinets, both of them with varying degrees of dents bashed into them.

I wondered how many of those dents were from everyday wear-and-tear and how many were the result of bouts of anger.

Or of a hostage's attempted escape . . .

The filing cabinets weren't locked and inside I found nothing much of interest: file upon file of financial statements, all those things that—*really*—I'd probably have needed an accountant holding my hand so that I might *begin* to understand them.

I looked about the inside of the filing cabinets, expecting to find—*perhaps*—a photograph, or a bloody lock of hair, or a hurriedly scrawled handwritten message wadged carelessly inside.

But, no, *nothing.*

I left the filing cabinets alone.

My streak of bad luck extended to the desk drawers.

Nothing there of any interest, although, inside one drawer, I did find about ten years' worth of calendars stacked up in a pile. They were all the same series, as far as I could tell. All of them entitled: *Beach Bums of the Year!!* . . . along with the corresponding year for each. When I glanced up, sure enough, I saw this year's calendar hanging down from a jagged nail, clearly hastily punched into the wall of the office.

A pair of plastic breasts—a plastic *smile*—stared right back at me.

The calendar was still stuck on Miss June, or whatever her name was—fully four months out of date—and I saw that there were several items marked in a childish scrawl alongside each of the days.

One word was repeated several times:

Shipment.

That sounded innocent enough . . . if a little vague.

Another entry read:

File accounts.

Another still:

Payroll.

It was clear that June wasn't getting me anywhere, so, increasing my grip on the torch, I flipped back the pages till I got to the current month.

October.

I wondered to myself whether the pages of the calendar had maybe slipped back to June as the result of a draught, or a slammed door, or if whoever this office pertained to had deliberately flipped the calendar back a few months in an attempt to ward off prying eyes.

Anything was possible.

I really had no idea of who I was dealing with here.

Drugs?

Guns?

. . . Something else?

Something *worse?*

To the unsuspecting eye, there would've been nothing at all curious about the month of October. There were all those same labels I'd seen before . . . from previous months.

However, one day of the month did stand out to me.

Because somebody had drawn a scruffy star around it in red pen.

The day was about two weeks before today's date.

I wondered if this might be the clue I'd waited for.

Outside the office, I heard a *Psst!* which I knew could only be Gemma telling me to hurry up. That somebody was coming. But I wouldn't be hurried.

Thinking quickly—I suppose its technical name is 'thinking on your feet'—I dashed back across the office to the filing cabinets.

I flipped through the files.

Through those cardboard stubs.

Looking—*desperately looking*—for something.

Finally, I found the month of October.

Not having any time to be discerning, I grabbed hold of the entire bunch of papers nestled within the cardboard divider.

I lugged them across the room, the torch batting light all around me, making me just a touch confused. More than a little delirious.

As I was coming out the door my foot searched for the step.

Couldn't find it.

Before I knew what was happening, I was tumbling.

A distant *thump.*

And then everything went black.

8

I CAME AROUND to the sound of hissing.

When I smelled the air, I was sure it was gas.

It had that same sharp quality to it.

The one which made me want to go and call the authorities.

. . . Which, in retrospect, I suppose, is the entire purpose of the smell . . .

My temple throbbed. It felt like there was a welt growing out of me.

The ground was hard beneath me.

I could feel it making my back numb.

My mind snapped back to what had just happened, how I had been prowling about the office of the warehouse.

The papers!

I had been grasping them so tightly that one of the papers had slipped out of its cardboard divide and sliced through my skin. I could feel the sharp pain coming from my arm. And I thought I could feel warm blood oozing out too.

I opened my eyes.

Bright—*bright!*—light.

I shut my eyes again.

This time I was more cautious. I opened my eyes only a crack. Allowed my pupils to get used to that much before risking opening them all the way.

Then the voice warbled about my brain.

And my mind slowly made sense of it.

The brash, brisk voice of Gemma.

"You all right?" Gemma said. "You took one hell of a fucking tumble."

I reached up and pressed my fingers—pleasantly cool because they were still covered by my leather gloves—to my temple.

Yep, it was going to be a real *shiner* by morning.

I knew I was going to get some looks off the general public . . . probably the only woman honestly able to say she actually *did* fall down a set of stairs.

"Where . . ." I just about got out, before my eyes stitched my surroundings together.

The booth.

The guard's booth.

Just beyond, I could see my car.

My vision blurred again.

There was something . . . there . . . on the windscreen?

Something beneath the windscreen *wiper* . . . or was my brain just all sozzled from the 'tumble' I'd taken down those steps?

I blinked several times, glanced back at Gemma.

All at once, sense seemed to return to me.

"Someone," I said, "someone was coming?"

Gemma gave me a wide grin and I saw that she had a few gold fillings towards the back of her mouth. She shrugged. "Sorry, false alarm. You know what it's like about here, all sorts of funny shit around." She twirled her finger up at her temple, as if to indicate madness. "Makes you see things sometimes."

"Yeah," I said, my mouth tasting incredibly dry, and my blood welling up into my temples, making the task of coordinating my brain and mouth very tricky indeed.

Another thought struck me.

I stared hard at Gemma.

Actually *startled* her a touch. "The papers?" I said. "Did you bring the papers with you?"

Gemma dug about on the little ledge, reaching for something beside her magazine which still lay opened flat there. She produced that familiar brown folder of papers I'd purloined from the office in the warehouse.

"There you go," she said, slapping them down on my stomach, while I continued to lie on my back.

As I straightened up, and, with Gemma's help, got back up onto my feet, I looked to the little electrical heater.

I guessed that was where the sound of hissing had come from, and, as for the smell of gas, I supposed my mind had just been playing tricks on me.

The heater was *very much* plugged into the electricity socket in the wall.

"That be all for this evening?" Gemma said, another wry smile for me.

I nodded back at her and tried my best to smile back, though I could feel the nausea pinching my stomach. It took a concentrated effort to clutch the folder of papers to my chest, to not let them slide through my grip and slap down onto the floor.

"Yes," I replied, finally, "I think so."

Gemma tapped the visor of her cap and then, with a wink, disappeared back inside her booth.

I walked back to my car, the thought of how she had managed to carry me—*unconscious*—back here all alone very much on my mind.

I guess, like a lot of security guards, she might've been packing quite a bit more muscle than I had bargained for.

I dumped the papers onto the passenger seat of my car, shut the door and then busied myself with the note which was stuck beneath my windscreen wiper.

It was written out in block capitals.

Very plain.

Easy to understand:

STAY AWAY

I glanced about me, at first convinced that somebody might be watching from the shadows. Once I'd contented myself that there was really nobody at all, I went to ask Gemma if she'd seen anybody lurking.

She hadn't.

So I wished her a good night, once again, and clambered back into my car.

Got back into the driver's seat.

And drove away.

9

I DECIDED to sleep on that whole experience at the River Gour.

My hearing was buzzing with invisible bees when I slumped down onto the well-beaten mattress of my bed, in my studio flat —a stone's throw away from my office.

And I didn't emerge from my pit until mid-morning the next day.

In fact, I could hardly believe the gleaming sunrays which penetrated the slatted wooden blinds of my bedroom. I had to actually bring my hand up to shield my eyes it was so bright. I vaguely wondered where that sun had been the day before, when I'd been down on the grim banks of the River Gour.

When I shrugged off the blankets of my bed, allowed them to tumble into a pile at my feet, I was immediately struck with— what seemed like—the Most Powerful Headache of All Time. It was like I'd been out all night drinking and then followed it up by banging my head against a brick wall.

I brushed my teeth contemplating the enormous bruise bursting out of my forehead and thinking about how easy it was to extract kindness from strangers with just a few well-placed quid.

I got myself showered and then dressed in one of the seven trouser suits I have for work—that day I went for mauve . . . it was that sort of a case.

Next, I turned my attention to the cardboard folder containing the papers for October.

As I sat down at the kitchen table, a cup of black instant coffee steaming away at my left elbow, I thought back to the note beneath my windscreen. The one which'd implored that I 'STAY AWAY.'

I wondered at what point it had been placed beneath the arm of the windscreen wiper.

Had it been while I'd been off at the warehouse office with Gemma?

Or had it been afterwards?

When I'd lain there, on the floor of the booth, mind slowly coming back to its senses.

Try as I might, I couldn't quite get a reasonable timeframe straight in my head.

But I attributed that, in part, to the bump on the head I'd got last night.

The papers nestled within the cardboard folder were Double Dutch to me.

All invoices.

Some with rubber stamps on them.

Dates.

Times.

Signatures.

I flipped through the paperwork and wondered if that trick Gemma had pulled with the camera in her booth had really removed the threat of discovery as completely as could be hoped.

Well, it was a little late for that now . . .

I recalled the date on the calendar, and I turned my attention to that.

Looked through the papers, skimming for that particular day.

Finally, I turned up a piece of paper which matched.

The only paper record for that day, in fact.

And even *I* could work out what it meant.

The page had a letterhead:

Fastmoore Shipping: International Delivery is our Priority!

I felt frown lines crease into my forehead.

On the invoice, I saw that there was a package listed.

It weighed 60 kilos.

Something sparked in my mind.

Why, a girl, about the age of my client, might weigh that.

With no other thoughts on my mind, I stood up quickly, knocking over my as-yet undrunk coffee with my elbow.

Sent the almost-boiling hot liquid spilling all over the other papers.

"Shit!" I let out.

Thankfully, as I mopped up the coffee with the now sopping-wet papers, the spillage didn't quite manage to reach the invoice I'd been interested in.

But, one thing was for certain, if I *had* wished to cart the papers back to the filing cabinet of that warehouse office, then that option was very much off the cards now.

It would be obvious somebody had tampered with the papers.

Deciding that I might as well cut my losses, I dumped the soiled papers in the kitchen bin, and then made a point of putting the *Fastmoore Shipping* invoice up on the counter, where it would be safe.

Safe from my clumsiness.

After that spot of drama, I made it to the phone.

I dialled up my client.

Couldn't get through.

And I wasn't in the habit of leaving voicemail messages.

Thinking quickly, I fished through my coat and uncovered the business card my client had handed me. It had the logo of the welding cooperative on one side; my client's name, and a mobile number, scrawled on the back in childish handwriting.

I plugged that information into my phone and saw that it'd be about a twenty-minute drive from my flat.

That done, I sailed on out through the door.

Down to my car.
And away to sniff out my lead.

10

THE WELDING COOPERATIVE was named, somewhat chippily:

Winders Welders

It was situated on another industrial estate, across the other side of town.

The other side of town to the River Gour.

The unit itself looked like it'd successively passed through the hands of just about every trade that existed, which was to say that the corrugated-iron frontage could've done with a lick of paint.

And the asphalt had been all torn up by decades of backing-up heavy goods vehicles.

The sliding door was about seven-eighths open and I could see the giveaway splash of sparks emanating from within. In the bright glow of a blowtorch—or whatever it was that the welders used—I made out the slightly eerie sight of a welder wearing a metal mask with one of those tiny, tinted, letterbox windows.

I got out my business card and asked after Paul.

The welder, who'd been working when I'd come in, was about sixty years old, with grey hair down to his shoulders, and a jolly beer gut which stuck out over the waistband of his overalls.

A well-soiled rag hung out of his back pocket.

As I spoke to him, he screwed up his eyes in a way that told me—*instinctively*—that either (a) he didn't believe that this was a place for a woman, or (b) that he just didn't much like women at all.

The welder scratched his balding scalp a pair of times and then bellowed out into the darkness of the workshop, before, promptly, and without another word to me, returning to his work.

Call me ignorant, but I couldn't see at all what the welder was working on.

To the untrained eye, it just looked like some scrap-metal poles with peeling black paint.

What their use could possibly entail escaped me.

Paul eventually emerged from the darkness, stifling a yawn with the back of his hand. When he realised it was me, though, he suddenly seemed to snap awake.

As if somebody had IV-ed him an espresso.

He padded up to me, nodding for the exit.

That we should go outside.

And since it was sunny out, and didn't stink of oil and *man* odour, I didn't complain.

First off, Paul pointed to his temple, obviously trying to communicate—in that *simian* way of manual labourers—that I had a boo-boo on my forehead.

I flashed my eyebrows at him. "Yeah," I said, "you should've seen the other guy."

By his wide-eyed gaze, I'm not totally sure he got the sarcasm . . .

I filled Paul in on what I had discovered the day before.

And what I had seen in the papers that morning.

He just stood there, open-mouthed, apparently unable to fathom just what I was saying.

All I was really hoping was that he might have a completion fee nearby.

Ready to hand over to his friendly, neighbourhood private investigator.

In the bright sunlight, Paul gaped at me. "Freight?"

"That's what I said."

"You mean, you think . . . that they sent . . . that they put . . ."

I nodded back at him.

Paul looked beyond me, shaking his head. He pressed his lips together, apparently in thought. I saw that he had a smudge of soot on his cheek and I had a somewhat motherly urge to spit on my finger and wipe it away.

But I restrained myself.

It's called *Being Pro* . . .

Paul shook his head some more and then turned back to me. "You any idea where they sent her?"

I reached into my coat, removed the invoice for the shipping and handed it to him.

For a second, the way he screwed up his eyes, I thought that he was going to ask me to read it to him. But apparently it was just his way of reading, because, about half a minute later he looked up over the invoice at me and said, "This don't look good, does it?"

I gave a shrug.

Paul read over the invoice another time. Then he looked to me again. "Have you been able to find anything else out?"

I shook my head. "The way I see it—if they've gone and sent her freight things slip just a little out of my jurisdiction unless you've got the . . ." and here I rubbed my thumb and forefinger together in what—in retrospect—must've seemed like an extremely sleazy gesture.

Paul didn't seem to find any sort of comedy, though, and he glanced over the invoice for a third, and final, time. "Nah," he said, handing the page back to me, as if I had any use for it, "I ain't got no money for that."

As Paul turned around, headed back into the workshop, I said, "That's that, then? I mean, you don't want me to look into this anymore?"

Paul stopped. He didn't turn around, but he tilted his head in my general direction. When he spoke, his voice sounded tired —*broken*, even. "Nah," he said. "Like you said, 'out of your jury-stic-shun.' "

And, with that, he disappeared back into the darkness of the workshop.

Left me to stand alone on the pavement outside.

I gave Paul a grace period of all of ten seconds, and then I returned to my car.

Immensely looking forward to an unexpected midday nap.

11

THE TROUBLE with going to bed in the middle of the day is that it wreaks havoc with your body clock . . . as I soon discovered when I lay in bed tossing and turning around the witching hours of the early morning the next day.

I finally cracked—*gave in*—got up and made myself some noodles.

They're good thinking food, or something . . .

I'd left the invoice on the kitchen table from the night before, at that moment too tired—my head too addled by the bump on my temple—to do anything more about it.

And looking it over again, in the wee hours of the morning, did little to advance my understanding of the whole case.

And—anyway—there *was* no case.

No client.

No money.

Equals:

NO CASE

But I couldn't stop the whole business from tumbling around my brain.

Contrary to popular belief, as a private investigator, I really don't spend all that much time rooting about private property *pilfering* documents: business, or otherwise.

Most of the work that I'd done up until that point had—almost exclusively—dealt with possible infidelities, or lost pets.

I have to admit that this case had done something to ignite that old girlish sleuth in me. The little voice which'd seen me wanting to take on the private investigator gig in the first place.

Perhaps the same little voice that'd quietly whispered me into flunking all those police exams.

I looked over the invoice form again, as if I was still getting paid to do so.

I tried to see something beyond the obvious stated weight and price information.

. . . And couldn't, really.

I *had* been staring at the invoice for an awfully long time.

Before I really knew what I was doing, I was throwing my coat over the shoulders of my pyjamas and shucking my slippers in favour of my rugged walking boots.

The ones that I'd taken down to the Gour last time out.

They were still caked in the muddy gunk from the bank.

In the night-time streets, it took me no time at all.

I could go just as fast as I wanted—within reason—to get to the Gour.

Soon enough, I found myself at the same spot with the security booth. Gemma inside. The girl from before. I could see through the illuminated window that she was slumped over on that little ledge-cum-desk thing which she'd been reading her magazine on.

But when I slammed the driver door shut, she stirred.

Raised her head as casually as if she'd been curled-up asleep on a Saturday morning. Her duvet gathered about her. Doing her best to see off the invasion of daylight.

She gave me the outline of a smile then rolled her shoulders, stifled a yawn with the back of her hand, and got up to her feet to meet me.

"Come to make another investment?" she said, arching an eyebrow, and—all at once—seeming awake and alert.

I smiled back at her. Then I shuffled through my pockets. Produced the invoice I'd swiped from the warehouse office. Handed it over to her.

At first, I thought that I was going to have to explain my chain of logic—just as I had had to do with my client . . . with

Paul the Welder—but she surprised me in blinking rapidly a couple of times then tilting her head to one side, narrowing her eyes as she handed the invoice back to me.

"You think they posted her?"

I nodded back. "Yeah, it's a working hypothesis."

"Hmm," Gemma said, glancing about the emptied car park of the industrial estate.

I wondered just *what* exactly it was that she was supposed to be protecting.

But I thought the question just a touch insulting so left it unasked.

When Gemma turned back to face me, she was wearing a wry smile. "You know what," she said, "think I might've heard something after all."

I felt my chest tighten.

I had brought along money.

Of course I had.

I wouldn't have bothered to come all the way out here—*in the middle of the night*—if I hadn't been prepared to bring along all the 'tools' that I might need to achieve my aims.

But I was wary.

The way this whole thing was playing out had a nasty smell to it—much like the stink of rat piss that carried on the night-time breeze over the Gour.

I looked to Gemma, half shutting one of my eyes in a way, I hoped, looked like I might know what I was doing here. "How'd I know that you'll give me some clue that I can use—what was stopping you from spilling the whole deal when I gave you that last hundred quid?"

I did it almost unconsciously, but I glanced over Gemma's shoulder to the surveillance camera there. The one which pointed back off behind us, towards the river. Its red light burning bright.

Very much *on* . . . or so it seemed.

Gemma followed my gaze. "No sound," she said, though she seemed a little shaken up by my gesture . . . enough so to suggest that she no longer believed herself to have the upper hand in this negotiation.

"So," I said, "how's about we do it a little differently this time?"

"How'd you mean?" she said.

"Well, let's just say that pay is *performance* based."

Her silence spoke volumes.

12

ALTHOUGH I HAD COME DRESSED for another *impromptu* trip down to the banks of the Gour, I was pleasantly surprised to see that that wasn't where we were headed.

Instead of Gemma letting us through the rusted-up, bolted-shut iron gate, she led me across the car park, where I had left my hatchback on my previous visit here, and over to a side door to one of the warehouses.

One of the warehouses it was Gemma's duty to protect.

She worked the keys over quickly through the padlock, but I wondered how long it might take her to jimmy it using that 'leaden-fingers-twisted' technique of hers.

Probably the same amount of time.

Inside the warehouse, the air stank of some sharp chemicals, and I was surprised to find that, as I took steps forwards, there was the *splash* of water beneath the tread of my boots.

Gemma turned back to me, her voice dropped to a whisper, and she said, "Not gonna switch on the torch here, there's cameras, all right? Not meant to be in here."

I signalled with an A-okay gesture, then she led us onwards.

She brought us through a series of boxes, all of them stacked, one upon the other, and then she stopped suddenly.

Or it *seemed* sudden to me given that I couldn't see a bloody thing.

Another *jingle-jangle* of keys later and the *clicking* of a lock being opened, a *bleep-blip* of a security alarm being activated and then, swiftly, disarmed; we stood within another office.

A bank of black-and-white TV monitors facing us down.

Setting me and Gemma in an eerie, silvery glow.

Gemma worked quickly, and without instruction.

She woke up a computer which'd been quietly sleeping and,

with a flurry of fingertips across the keyboard, she made one of the black-and-white monitors flicker away from the present security film and into an almost blinding *white* static.

That lasted only a couple of moments because no sooner had Gemma tapped at the computer than the monitor flickered.

Froze the frame.

The date stamped there at the bottom.

The same date as had been written on the invoice.

In the ethereal half-light, I looked to Gemma.

Gemma just nodded back at me, ducked down and tapped about with the computer keyboard another thousand times.

The image began to move.

Slowly.

Slowed down to at least four times normal speed.

It was *clearly* the feed from the security camera which hung from the guard booth. The one which pointed off down at the river. And it was a good thing too because—right now—I could, as plain as day, see the pair of men I'd seen walking along the bank before carrying a package . . . a *cloth* bag? . . . it was causing them some discomfort.

I glanced to Gemma, then back to the camera.

It remained fixed on the men till they slipped out of frame.

For what seemed like an eternity, I was speechless.

In the end, it was Gemma who broke the silence.

"Want me to run it a few hours later?"

"Yes," I said.

13

E VERYTHING WAS RIGHT THERE—all the evidence, everything that might be needed to prove the kidnapping. About an hour later on the footage, a small ship arrived to the dock of the warehouse me and Gemma had broken into. Although the men were only half in frame, it was clear to see the two of them lugging a box onto the back of the ship.

Since the box was made of wood, there was no sign of any struggle inside, though, for my money, they would've made sure to drug their victim before confining her to that journey.

Once loaded onto the back of the ship, and with the men retreating back to the warehouse—but not without them giving a clear shot of their faces—the ship chugged on off, up the river.

Away from the warehouse.

Its cargo destined for some location.

Far away.

The two of us watched the camera feed turn back to showing only the River Gour. Even in black and white it was clear to see that it wasn't much to look at, to put it mildly.

I couldn't help but feel a question lodged in my brain.

The one which I was desperate to ask of Gemma.

Thankfully, though—*mercifully*—she seemed to read my mind.

"You wanna know why I didn't come in here before," she said, "why I didn't do some investigating for myself?"

I nodded back at her, feeling a touch glum.

"Listen," she said, her eyes still fixed on the now-featureless feed from all those weeks ago, "what I told you before, about how I do what they ask me to do—nothing else?"

Again, I nodded.

"I wasn't trying to pull the wool over your eyes. The stuff that I hear, the stuff that I *see* . . . well, truth be told, that's not the half of what goes on . . . I get paid for security, to look over this place. To keep it safe overnight."

Her words seemed to create an echoplex within my brain.

It made them almost impossible to put into place.

To put into order.

But then it struck me.

I felt a sharp pang at the base of my gut.

"The note," I said, "the one on my windscreen?"

She gave me a dour nod.

"You wrote it . . ." I added, unnecessarily.

Gemma gave a vague shrug, pouted a little, and then said, "Can't blame a girl for trying to make her life easier, huh?"

I felt numb for a few seconds, and then I thought to respond.

"No," I replied, "I suppose you can't."

14

WITH THE EVIDENCE ALL READY—and with Gemma well-taken care of, well *compensated* for her part in all this . . . it'd taken my entire fee, and then some—we turned the whole lot into the police.

And since I no longer had a client paying my way, I saw no reason *not* to go against his wishes.

I did the Right Thing.

Or so it seemed.

Although the police had no need to, they kept me in the loop as much as they were able.

Told me that they had passed the information onto their International Crimes Unit.

And that they expected results in the near future.

Yeah, had I ever heard *that* one before . . .

But, true to their word, about a week after I'd handed over the evidence, I came back home, after an uneventful—and *unsuccessful*—attempt at tracking down a Labrador puppy for my latest client, I found that I had a new voicemail message.

Knowing that it wasn't likely to be a follow-up from the three first dates I'd been on that month, I prepared myself for what was—*surely*—going to be some sort of a threat.

In actual fact, I was getting a little excited about it.

I suppose that—for a private investigator—receiving hate mail is just about the highest form of flattery.

But it was from the police.

They informed me that they had located the kidnapped girl, and that she had been sold into white slavery. Into one of those *infamous* international brothels. My contact, apparently in a talkative mood, went on to say that they had rounded up all those responsible from the warehouse, and they had them in custody.

They wanted me to 'swing by'—his words, not mine—so that I could corroborate some vital pieces of evidence.

What else could a girl say?

I couldn't exactly turn them down, could I?

So, with a slight smile on my lips, and remembering, pretty much as I stood with my thumb on the latch to my door, I swiped up a handful of business cards to take along with me.

Yeah, business cards.

That was the trick to professionalism.

If I still had anything to prove at all:

Auburn Spector, Private Investigator.

SNAIL TRAIL

R YAN SCUFFS HIS SHOES against the curb as he
meanders toward the job centre. Already he can see the
queue curling its way along the pavement. He got up late again
this morning, despite setting his alarm for seven, he slept right
through it, only getting up at half nine. If he doesn't get his eight
hours of sleep he gets all groggy the next day, and it's not like
dropping off to sleep is easy either. It takes a muted TV, splashing
vapid, multi-coloured images over him, and a handful of
painkillers to get him to sleep around one am. And then it's not
like real sleep—it's a dull, empty approximation. There's no
room for dreams. Just vague shapes and formless faces. And then
he wakes.

He jiggles a squashed pack of cigarettes out of his jacket
pocket. He looks at the low definition image of a diseased lung
on the front, with its smug message:

Smoking may cause lung cancer.

Does whoever created that message think that he doesn't
know that? Do they really think that he smokes to be *cool*? He
flips the lid and jabs one of the crooked cigarettes between his
lips and lights it with the cheapo orange lighter with a roaring
tiger slapped on the side. He sucks on the cigarette and eyes the
queue up ahead as it snakes forward, one person at a time
crossing the threshold into the job centre.

Once inside he gets the typical form which asks him, in
simple English—English that the *unemployed* will understand—
which applications he's made in the last week, what he's done in
exchange for his state-tossed scrap, the *job seekers'* allowance. He
answers, honestly, that he's made twenty-six applications, been
called for six interviews. All the outcomes have come to nought,
just as they always do.

He waits for his turn for the kindly, grey-haired lady with the golden broach—which suggests she might be doing this job as some sort of hopped-up community service, that she's got a husband who's perhaps working in the city, while she fritters away for something to make her life more worthwhile—as she clutches her clipboard to her sagging chest and calls out names for their interview.

When Ryan's name pops up, he puts down the pamphlet he was reading on opportunities abroad and he trots past the lady, giving her a slight grin, before shutting the door behind him and taking up his place on the plastic-feeling fire-red sofa opposite his employment adviser. A new one. Different from last week. The job turnover rate here is through the roof. Another face every month or so.

She cocks her head to one side and examines his filled out form, looking over the appropriate fields. She glances up to him and gives him an easy smile. "You've got very tidy handwriting."

"Thanks," Ryan says, doing his best not to smirk.

She nods as she goes through all the information, then taps her pen twice against her thigh before saying, "You've certainly been busy. Shame that nothing's come up."

"Isn't it?"

"Says here that you applied to *Brollison's Deli*, that you got an interview there." She glances up at him. "Like to tell me what happened?"

Ryan shrugs. "Someone else got the job."

"And do you think there's anything you might've done better?"

"No."

"You sound quite certain."

"I am."

"Why's that, then?"

"Just don't think anyone'd be interested in taking me on."

"But you've got skills"—she peers down at the CV which Ryan notices she keeps in her lap—"you've got a degree in aero-nautical engineering . . . from *Batsley University*." She looks at him again. "Not everyone can say that, I'm sure. What I wouldn't give to have studied there."

"Yeah, I know, I've been lucky in life, I suppose."

She scoffs. "Luck doesn't have anything to do with getting accepted at *Batsley*. You've got to have some serious brains going on to get in there."

Again, Ryan shrugs.

She sighs. "Well, I can see that you're trying. I wish there was some little titbit I could give you, some advice on where you might be going on. But someone with your brains is far ahead of me, I'm sure of that."

Ryan stays quiet.

She squints and bites into her lower lip. She looks at him once, then another couple of times before parting her mouth. "Have . . . have I seen you somewhere before?"

Ryan sniffs, waiting for her to make the connection. They always do. He doesn't want to prompt her because he always has fresh hope that they won't work out who he is—what's gone on in his past—but, at the same time, he doesn't want to be rude by making some excuse and bounding out. He knows he has to head this off, be proactive. If he gets to the point where he can no longer face it, it will have won.

She continues to think the matter over and then says, "I saw you in the news. In all the papers. With that . . ."

"It's okay," he says. "You can say it."

"With that, mugger. On the bus. You . . . you killed him."

Ryan remains still. Every time he thinks it in his mind even if they don't dare say it to his face. *Murderer*. That's what he is. No getting away from it. He fiddles with his hands, not wanting to subject her to the awkwardness of having to meet his eye.

"No," she says. "Sorry, that came out all wrong. I mean, from what I read, you were a hero. You saved all those people."

"Uh huh."

"But, I read . . . that they wanted to lock you up. I remember those passengers, all those families, they all protested, and you got off the hook. Not guilty. The judge said that you were a *hero*, that you stepped in where others never would have. But, that . . . that . . ."

Ryan knows how she wants to follow this up. She wants to say that he used 'unreasonable force' that after the fifth or sixth punch he should've stopped. He'd got the poor bugger pinned by his chest after all. He wasn't getting away. But a thin, crimson veil had drifted down over his eyes. And, as he pointed out to himself, no one had said anything, made any move to stop him—to tell him what he was doing was wrong.

He still remembers the faces of the coppers who took him away. How they'd put him in handcuffs. He recalls the gentle, congratulatory tap on the shoulder from the constable when he arrived at the police station. They had to do their jobs, but they were sure, from what they'd put together from the witnesses, that Ryan had done the right thing.

The moral thing.

"Can you talk about it?" she says.

"A bit."

"What happened?"

Ryan runs his tongue round his teeth, feeling for the grainy stretches of plaque. He unknots his hands and looks her right in the eye. "I'm sure you read all about it. In the paper."

"Yeah," she says, with a slight smile, "but you know how the papers are, twisting everything round till it doesn't resemble much of anything anymore."

"He had a gun. That's all I know. I just flipped, like a light

152

clicked on in my brain. I knocked him down before he could shoot."

"So he was a mugger, then?"

"Don't know."

"Never got a chance to question him, I suppose?"

"No."

She remains deeply focussed on him, as if some invisible thread ties her pupils to his. "I just don't see why you're finding it hard to get a job. Everyone should be chomping at the bit to take someone like you on."

"Should they?"

"Well, yeah."

"Right," he says, getting fidgety.

A few moments later she remembers herself and scrabbles through a filing cabinet at her side. She flips through the files, withdraws one and then slides Ryan's completed sheet from that week inside. She crosses and then uncrosses her legs. "Guess I'll see you same time next week, then."

"If you're still here."

"If you don't get a job."

Ryan nods to her in acknowledgement and gets up. He heads for the door, twists the knobs and then wanders out through the job centre past all the others waiting there—the middle-aged men in their tracksuit bottoms, the teenage mothers with baby's sleeping in their arms, the recently graduated students looking twitchy, as if they might be about to be jumped on from any side. The room's a cacophony of perfume, week-old beer and body odour. It's that smell which drives Ryan out into the street, the one which plagues his mind as he lights up his cigarette.

As he strides off along the street in the direction of the municipal park, he passes late stragglers, others heading into the job centre. He averts his gaze. It doesn't happen often in the street—people don't recognise him and stop him right there—but he can't be a hundred per cent sure.

When he gets into the park, he picks out a pleasant wooden bench dedicated to someone's dead grandfather and he blows out the smoke in a long, continuous stream. It's a beautiful day: azure sky, birds singing, leaves rustling in a light breeze. And then, all of a sudden, he gets the shakes. He has to put out his cigarette. He chews on his tongue, telling himself he's not going to cry. He's bigger than this. He'll get over it. One little episode and, anyway, what he did was right. Everyone says so. But he still sees it. In their eyes. They're afraid of him. And they always will be, or until they forget anyway. When will they stop being afraid? When he's dead? No, he can't think like that. He has to be positive.

He waits out the rest of the day in the park, not daring to move until the sun dips on the horizon, until night's sneaking up on the world. Darkness is his friend. It keeps the secret in his face safe, covers the oozing snail trail which leaks out from the soles of his shoes. He will find something, someday. Just like the girl at the job centre said, he's a hero.

Isn't he?

SCRAPE

1

I T FELT LIKE SOMEBODY held a naked flame to the thigh of his jeans.

Jacob could feel the blood soaking the material.

He could *smell* it on the stale, winter's night air.

And he could hear the *thump-thump* of his heart in his eardrums.

In the whole rush of the last couple of minutes, Jacob had bitten his tongue, and he could now taste blood in his mouth too. That harsh, coppery taste that sent chills down his spine.

He felt his legs finally give way and he fell, face down into a puddle, down *hard* onto the broken concrete of the side alley, nestled in darkness.

As Jacob hit the ground, he felt Trance—his best friend—grab hold of the sleeve of his hooded sweatshirt. But Trance couldn't stop him from striking hard.

The pain in Jacob's leg was just too much to bear now.

"Come on, buddy," Trance said, "gotta get outta here, yeah?"

Though Jacob heard the words rattle about his brain, he couldn't find the strength within himself to act of them. The pain was too much now. It was so severe that he couldn't so much as hear himself think. All that occupied his mind was the sensation of the blood pouring out of his thigh. He bit his tongue again and tasted a fresh wave of blood.

Trance tried to lift Jacob, but Jacob resisted him, made himself a deadweight—impossible for Trance to get off the ground. "Come on, buddy, come on," Trance said again, as if those motivational words would have more of an effect this time around.

They didn't.

As Jacob lay there, the blood pouring out from his thigh, he felt Trance move him around so that he no longer lay on his front, so that he lay on his back instead. From this position, Jacob could look up through the break in the rooftops above, and see the gentle sheen of stars all peering down on him.

Jacob's chin stung too, now, and he knew that, when he'd fallen, he'd smashed his chin against the tarmac also.

Trance was still gripping tight to Jacob's sweatshirt. "Come on, mate, let's get moving, then we'll get you all patched up, okay?"

Jacob just lay there, knowing that he could no longer put any weight whatsoever onto his leg . . . not unless he wanted to end up in a heap all over again.

Trance glanced back over his shoulder, and when he spoke again, his voice was much harder, unrelenting. "Mate, I can hear them coming—if you can't shift yourself then I'm gonna have to leave you, you don't want that, do ya?"

Jacob couldn't reply. He could feel all the warmth leaving his cheeks—all the *blood* leaving his cheeks—and he knew that, pretty soon, he would black out and collapse right here. Already he could feel himself sinking as if into a stodgy, gooey mess.

Jacob felt Trance's grip on him slipping, and Jacob could hear the footsteps just as well as Trance could. And it happened, just like that, Trance let Jacob go, allowed him to tumble down to the tarmac. All Jacob heard, as he lay on his side, was the *slap* of trainers on concrete.

And then silence.

2

"**O**I, THIS 'IM?"

Jacob heard the words dribble through his brain. He wasn't quite sure what to make of them. He had been dreaming —dreaming about something else, about *being* somewhere else— and now he was right back here.

In this side alley.

It had been raining. Jacob could smell it on the air. He could smell how grimy sewage had blended in with the falling water, how it had collected into puddles about him. He could feel that his clothes, too, were damp with rainwater. The salty taste in Jacob's mouth seemed to suggest to him that he had been crying . . . but if he had been *crying* then it would've been in his sleep . . . because Jacob had never *once* consciously cried . . . not in his life.

The pain in his leg seemed to have turned from searing and unbearable to almost totally numb. It now felt like his leg was nothing more than chilled, unfeeling flesh. When he tried to move his leg, he found that he couldn't.

He wondered how bad his injury really was.

Jacob felt them coming closer—the ones who'd happened on him here, in this side alley.

One of them nudged him in the side with his foot.

Jacob hissed in a lungful of air.

"Yeah," another voice said, "this's him—give us a hand, will ya, Rory?"

Jacob held himself still. He would've resisted if he'd still had any sort of strength, but the truth was that it'd all been sucked right out of him. It was almost as if his blood was his strength, and now that his blood lay about him in puddles he had it no longer.

Jacob felt them lifting him up to his feet. His head felt

unwieldy on the end of his neck, and it flopped forwards, down onto his chest.

The two men's grip was strong, though, and he could feel that they had a good hold on him. Jacob bet that, even at full strength, he might've had some trouble in breaking free of them. In fact, he admitted that it would've been almost impossible.

Bet . . . *bet* . . . that word rattled through Jacob again, and again, and again . . . because that was what Jacob had been up to with Trance, the two of them . . . they'd wanted . . . they'd *tried* . . . to rip off . . . to rip off . . . the . . . the game.

Jacob felt his mind flushing away.

Darkness returned.

3

W HEN JACOB SNAPPED TO, he could feel his buttocks numbing against a hard, flat surface. He blinked. He cast a bleary eye about himself, trying to absorb his surroundings. The gloom seemed to ebb away from him, to skulk in the shadows, just for a moment. Nothing more.

Because the gloom returned.

As far as Jacob could tell, he was inside of a tiny, windowless room. The air smelled of disinfectant and there was a sharp taste of stale blood in Jacob's mouth. Jacob remembered his tongue, how he'd bitten his tongue while he and Trance had been fleeing.

They'd had to run.

There'd been no other choice.

They'd blown it right open.

Nearby, Jacob could hear water dripping.

He glanced about himself, realised that he was parched.

He searched for the source of the water.

But he couldn't find it.

As the sound was beginning to drive Jacob crazy, he heard solid footsteps coming from somewhere. Jacob tried to move his hands, to bring them out before him so that he might block a coming blow. So that he might keep them from doing him more harm.

But he realised that his hands were held behind his back, that they had been tied up tight with a rough rope.

The numbness in Jacob's leg was complete now—he might as well have just had somebody's cast-off leg taped to his hip and have been over with it.

Jacob turned his attention in the direction of the footsteps.

They stopped when they reached the door.

What Jacob *believed* to be the door.

And when the footsteps paused, and when the hinges squealed, Jacob saw, right away, that he had been wrong. That while he had visualised—*imagined*—the door to be positioned in the wall right before him, it was in fact around to his side.

Strong, orange light splashed into the room.

Jacob found it blinding.

It torched his eyes.

Jacob breathed in deeply, trying to get himself back into his mind. To get himself back to thinking straight. He could see a shadowy figure standing in the doorway. A *large* figure.

Did he stand there with his hands in his pockets?

Yes, it seemed like he had his hands in his pockets.

As Jacob's eyes grew accustomed to the sharp light, he took in the details. How the figure was—clearly—a man, and how he wore a baggy suit, hands stuffed into his pockets, apparently to conceal the rest of his body.

It was only when the man spoke that Jacob reached any kind of inkling that this wasn't a man at all . . . that from the light tone in the gruff voice he *knew* it was a woman.

"Why'd you run?" the woman in the baggy suit said.

Jacob felt his mind flexing. He imagined a saturated sponge, encased in his skull, and that just to get an answer from himself he had to *squeeze* and *squeeze* hard.

It was a good thing that the woman continued speaking, because when Jacob opened his mouth to reply, he found that his tongue was dry and unwieldy.

"You and your friend," the woman said, taking a couple of steps into the room—into the gloom—"You show up at the blackjack and you think that you're just gonna sweep us all off the table, that what you thought, huh?"

Jacob said nothing in reply.

"You come there with some sorta strategy? Thought you were

gonna count cards or some shit? Like you were gonna do it just like they do on TV—in the movies?"

Jacob felt his chest tighten, and he felt his spine stiffen. More than anything he wanted to reach down for his leg, to feel if it was still there, or to see if—somehow—these people had sawed it off while he'd been blacked out, and somehow kept him alive.

Even in the dazzling light, Jacob could see that the woman was shaking her head, that her *silhouette* was shaking its head. "Nah, we saw you coming a mile off—you think that a pair of upstarts like the two of you hit us unexpected?" The woman was smiling now, Jacob could hear it in her voice. "Nah, happens maybe once a month. Pair of young kids with no patience. They see the game and they know they got to take chances. What they don't understand is this ain't no world of individual geniuses. Truth be told, geniuses are somewhat tough to come by . . . and you kids always think you're so smart."

Out of the gloom, Jacob heard the woman scratching at what sounded like stubble, but he was sure that it *couldn't* be stubble. It was only when Jacob blinked, when he brought the room into some new sort of a focus that he realised that the woman had stepped closer to him.

That she now stood *before* him.

Though Jacob felt his blood all pump to his head, he managed to keep himself from calling out—from shouting out in fright.

"Listen here, huh," the woman continued, "what happened here tonight was both very common and very rare. The common part is like I said before—that a pair of dummards like you two gets it into their minds to make a grab for our game—the *rare* part, though, is when one of the two manage to get away with the loot. That, I assure you, Mr Peterson"—the fact that the woman knew Jacob's surname sent a thrill through him—"does not happen often. Not at all. But when it does, you've gotta understand that there are *bad* things coming. Bad things for just about everybody involved."

Jacob sensed that the woman was closer still now.

His suspicion was confirmed by her strong, oniony breath.

And then by her sure hold of his testicles.

Jacob felt the pain spurt through him as she gripped his balls tight in her hand—with the same amount of brute force that a well-trained Alsatian might exert.

"You listen here, Mr Peterson, you're gonna help us get that money back what you stole, and you're gonna do it today, you hear?"

Jacob could already feel himself slipping away.

Leaving the woman again.

And—just like that—as if somebody had clicked their fingers, the lights went out.

4

WHEN JACOB AWOKE the light was blinding. And white. Direct sunlight. Had he truly believed that he would see the sun again?

Jacob could hear birdsong. Could feel a fresh, gentle, warming breeze up against his skin. And his mouth no longer tasted of blood, it tasted neutral, as if he'd bitten into a piece of smoothed-over rubber. He could smell the outside. The grass. The leaves. The *trees.*

Jacob found himself lying on a doctor's examination table. He was wearing a patient's gown, one of those synthetic materials that seemed to bake him like tinfoil about a potato. He listened to the plasticky paper sheet crinkle beneath his weight. He glanced about him. To the various surgical implements which stood off on the side of the counter.

Scalpels.

Scissors.

A rubber mallet for testing reflexes.

Jacob fantasised about making a grab for one or all of them. He told himself that he could escape, until he realised that there was another person in this room with him. Not like he had feared, the woman in the baggy suit from before, but somebody standing with their back to him, staring out through the window.

The person sensed Jacob stirring because they turned around, and Jacob saw that it was another woman. An *attractive* woman who wore a clean, green paper apron, and who had a bobbed, white-blond haircut. She was slightly tanned and Jacob wondered if she'd recently been on holiday. She gave him a faint smile, and then said, "Feeling better?"

Jacob couldn't answer right away. His first thought was for his leg. He reached down for it, touched it, and before he could get through his mind just what had gone on, the woman standing there answered for him.

"Fixed it up fine," she said, "just a few stitches here and there. You were lucky, the blade wasn't far off hitting an artery."

Jacob's mind blurred. He found that he could suck up the strength to speak now. "How . . . how . . ."

"How'd I know it was a blade?" she said, with another calming smile. "I know because of the form of the cut—of how it left your skin."

Jacob thought that sounded right—at least it seemed to square with most of the stuff he heard on TV or in movies. "Where . . ." Jacob got out.

"You're in a private institution, Mr Peterson," the woman went on, "and I've just finished patching you up so that whoever brought you here, to me, can take you off home again."

It was at that point when Jacob realised that the woman was a doctor—why hadn't he thought that before? Had he thought that she was a nurse? . . . No, he hadn't even thought that, he had just believed that she had been . . . how should he put this without sounding like a total nutter even inside of his own brain? . . . an *angel?*

"It was just a scrape, really," the woman, the *doctor* went on. This time her smile faded away completely. "Look, Mr Peterson, you don't have to tell me exactly what went on, but bear in mind that you *can* tell me if you believe yourself to be in danger. Are you in danger, Mr Peterson?"

Jacob found his mind skip a little. He recalled the gloomy room. The woman in that baggy suit of hers. He managed a skittish shake of the head. "No," he said, and then, a little more securely, "*No.*"

"Okay, Mr Peterson," the doctor said, in a voice which really didn't inspire any confidence, "then just lie back and I'll give you a sedative."

Once more, the world faded away.

5

NEXT THING JACOB KNEW, he found himself in the back of a car. The car had tinted-out windows and smelled of furniture polish and leather. He could feel the cotton ball inside of his mouth which the doctor had given him to chew so as to keep the wound on his tongue from weeping.

Jacob felt around him. He padded the leather seat he sat on. And he could feel a slight chill creeping into the back of the car.

On instinct, feeling that somebody was watching him, he glanced up.

And he saw her.

The woman from that gloomy room, that cellar, that basement, whatever it had been, the one who had squeezed his balls in her fist.

Jacob was a little worried that she might do it again.

But he did his best not to show his fear.

Now he could see the woman's face clearly, he realised that she kept her greying brown hair cropped short, and that she had a thick scar on her left cheek, one of those scars which looked like it had been made many, many years before. The skin was all hard and shiny, and a pinkish colour.

She wore the same suit from the night before—it *had* been the night before?—and she didn't turn to meet his eye. She just kept on facing forwards as she spoke to him. "Now, Jacob," she said, using his Christian name for the first time, "You're going to go and see your friend, and you're going to bring back what's rightly ours."

Jacob sat still in the seat. He felt almost as if somebody had set a plank of wood up against his spine. He glanced out at the passing greenery, dulled by the tinted-out windows. When he turned back to look at the woman, he saw that she still didn't look at him.

"You have until midnight tonight. If, by then, you fail to bring us your friend and everything—*everything*—that was stolen, then we shall come for you." The woman did turn to face Jacob now, and he found himself focussing in hard on the scarred side of the woman's face. He almost lost himself down that chapped and charred crack in her skin. "Somebody will die for what happened last night, Jacob, you'd just better hope that it's not you."

The car screeched to a halt on a street corner.

The woman was shoving a scrap of paper at him with a mobile number on it. "Any trouble, and you give me a call, okay?"

The lock on the door clicked open and Jacob took this as his cue to step out of the car.

Jacob only realised the million questions he had on his mind when he watched the back end of the car swing around the corner, and out of sight.

But, really, the only thing that mattered—the only thing he had to understand—was that he had to bring Trance, and all the money, to them by tonight.

Else they'd kill him.

6

JACOB LIMPED HIS WAY back to his apartment, in his dumpy neighbourhood, not much more than takeaway restaurants and dingy side alleys. But it was cheap, and that was what mattered. Inconspicuous, or so he'd hoped. And not that it mattered either seeing as he believed just what that woman had said to him, about them coming for him if he failed to bring back what was stolen.

When Jacob had made himself a pot of coffee, and drunk his way through it, he checked out the gash on his leg, and saw that it was nice and patched up by the pretty lady doctor. He wondered if he was getting his normal snap back—if he'd shaken off the fear and pain he had found himself enveloped in the night before.

But, when he went to place his emptied coffee cup in the sink, he watched on as it trembled in his grip, and came to an unsteady rest.

Because Jacob knew what he had to do.

That he had to bring those people Trance.

Or they'd do him.

This was survival.

Plain and simple.

He did want to *survive,* didn't he?

7

JACOB PLUCKED OUT his mobile from a drawer in the kitchen. He had had the good sense not to go to the blackjack game with his mobile on him. It would've been too risky. What if it had gone off at the wrong moment, or if he'd somehow left it behind? That would've let them know exactly who he was . . . and yet, he knew now, that they'd known all along just who he was. And there seemed nothing he could do to stop them.

Jacob rang up Trance more than a dozen times before he got anything other than his answerphone.

"Jay?"

Jacob could hear the strain in Trance's voice, and Jacob couldn't help wondering if Trance had sweated just what he'd done all night.

"Jay? That you, Jay?"

Jacob held back still, not wanting to utter so much as a word yet.

And then, just like that, Jacob hung up.

Jacob held his mobile to his neck, as if it might help him to think straight.

What was he doing?

Could he *really* hand over his best friend in the whole world just to save his own skin?

A slight throb of pain in his leg brought him back to his senses.

Trance had left him, had left him in the side alley.

Had left him to be caught.

But had Trance had any other choice?

If Trance hadn't fled then they both—along with the money —would've been grabbed.

What was the right way out of this for Jacob?

How could he square this with himself?

Live with himself afterwards?

Because Jacob was many things, but he could hardly ever lower himself to the level of simple liars.

Not unless he could trick *himself* in some way.

Thinking quickly, Jacob dipped his hand into the pocket of his jeans, retrieved the scrap of paper from within—the one which the woman had given him before promptly turning him out of her car. He thought long and hard, and then he'd got it.

The answer.

The only way he'd be able to do it.

8

TWO HOURS LATER, Jacob stood in a trench coat, his collar turned up to shield his neck from the chilly breeze which ran along the main street of Trance's neighbourhood. He had a scarf up to cover his nose and mouth too, and a beanie cap pulled down over his head. He didn't look conspicuous seeing as everybody else was dressed in some similar cold-weather attire.

The only thing which *did* make him seem conspicuous was the way that Jacob hung about at the shop front of a tailor's. He could almost feel the mannequins, inside the shop window, outfitted in various dresses and suits, and all else, staring into his back.

Jacob had toyed with the idea of staying behind in his own apartment—not bothering to venture on out. Because it would be over soon enough. And Jacob had made it so that he didn't have to dirty his own hands. He had covered his tracks.

It was clear that Trance and him had been amateurs, and these guys had seen right through them. Trance had run off back home with the goods and all the woman, and whoever was behind her, needed to know was just where Trance lived.

That was *all* they needed.

Jacob stared at the entrance to Trance's apartment.

A steel door with an old-style, lock-and-key arrangement. There were several flyers all pasted up against the door which'd become worn and torn in the rain and wind, and which now resembled papier-mâché more than anything else.

It all happened so quickly.

The world just seemed to jump into life.

A car—the same one from that morning?—pulled up outside of Trance's place, and a pair of big men got out from either side.

They rang the bell to Trance's apartment a couple of times, and then they stood back, waiting for Trance to open up.

When Trance did, he blinked in the harsh winter sunlight of the afternoon.

Neither of the men laid hands on him, they simply led Trance, with his plastic bag snug in his hands, into the back seat of the car.

Jacob knew that he should go—that he should blow the scene—but he couldn't find the strength to feel the pain ripple up through his leg once more. So he stood still, and he watched on as the car ploughed on past him. And, just for a second, Jacob caught sight of Trance, staring out through the window, right at him.

Their eyes buzzed as they crossed.

Jacob was sure of it.

Some sort of a static electricity passing between their eyeballs.

And then, just like that, Trance was gone.

Jacob set off for home.

9

WHEN JACOB GOT BACK to his apartment, he found that the lock had been busted off the door. He should've run, should've tried to take off, and maybe he would've done so if it hadn't been for the pair of cars—one on each side of the street—lurking there.

Jacob wondered if he should've felt tricked, if he should've felt betrayed in some way, but, in the end, he just felt exhausted. He felt ready to just give into them.

For this all to be over.

As Jacob climbed the stairs to his apartment, he heard the woman's cough before he got to see her. When Jacob stepped in through the doorway, he caught sight of the woman standing at his sink, staring into it, down at the coffee cup he'd left there earlier.

She tilted her head back and looked at him with a crooked smile. "Nice idea," she said, "Telling your mate that we'd let you go if he only handed himself and the money in." She held her arm up to the daylight which dribbled in through the window and she inspected the cuff of her suit jacket for a moment. "And I bet you had half a thought that we might actually do just that."

No, Jacob wanted to answer, *Not really.*

The woman squared her shoulders, squeezed her fingers into fists, making the joints crack. She drew in a deep breath, her ribcage rising up as she did so, and then she said, "Ready to go?"

Jacob glanced around at the apartment, and knew this would be the last time.

When he glanced back at the woman he did feel sort of prepared.

This was the way they were *meant* to go . . . the way that he and Trance were *supposed* to be punished for what they'd done.

Together.

SNAPPING TEETH

1

THE WALLS of the dentist's office were an off white. A plastic plant sat in the corner of the waiting room, apparently wilting, while a new secretary tapped away at her keyboard. She had blond hair and paused every few seconds to tuck a strand of it behind her ear.

Derek strode up to the desk and laid his palm flat on the plastic surface, sending his gold chain rattling. "What happened to the old secretary?"

"Sorry, sir?"

"The last secretary. Old girl."

She blinked a couple of times.

"It's just strange. I've been coming here for over twenty years and she's been here every time."

"Really?"

His heart beat faster. He glanced about. There was something wrong about all this. Today, ever since he'd woken up this morning with a hardness in his mouth, like kernels of wheat between his teeth, everything had been wrong. Someone after him. He felt it in his bones.

"Sir?"

He looked back at her, trying to refocus, to get a grip on himself. Perhaps he was just being paranoid. He draped his tongue about his lips and showed his top row of teeth. "Name's Derek Wrombsford. Got an appointment with Mr Morris."

She clicked her mouse. "Eleven thirty?"

"Yes."

"Take a seat, please. Mr Morris is just getting ready."

Some recognition sparked in his mind. Déjà vu? He kept his eyes fixed on her. "Have I seen you before?"

She rolled out a drawer and flicked through a set of yellowing files. "No, sir. I don't think so."

"You look so familiar."

She glanced up and smiled. "I get that quite a lot."

He lingered another moment then selected the chair with the least amount of foam poking out from it. Magazines lay fanned out on the coffee table. He scanned the covers, settling for the one with the biggest pair of breasts.

Leafing through, he considered the secretary. He was sure she was lying to him. To be in his line of work it was necessary to know how to judge people. Perhaps she was a stripper or a prostitute. He'd worked with enough. All their faces got familiar after a while, blended into one. That must've been it. He'd bumped into girls who'd worked for him on the streets and they were always eager to look away, to forget their past lives.

He glanced up at the clock and sighed. Sometimes he thought what he did was a thankless task, putting people back on their feet from their lowest point. Jesus, he was a superhero. After this appointment he'd head off to one of his massage parlours. Cheer himself up.

A speaker crackled behind the secretary. The dentist's voice. "Mr Wrombsford. Eleven thirty."

Derek set the magazine down and took a quick lungful of air. He wiped his clammy palms on his trouser pockets and walked past the secretary, who didn't look up from her computer screen. It made him smile.

The stairs was narrow and steep, and there was no banister. He climbed the stairs one at a time, running his hands along the scuffed walls for support. When he reached the top, he rapped his knuckles against the door.

"Come in."

Derek readjusted the waistband of his jeans, tucking his shirt in further, and stepped inside.

Morris wore a white jacket and faced away from Derek, slouching over a set of drawers. "Sit down, please."

A reclining brown leather chair stood in the centre of the room with a cream spotlight towering above. It reminded Derek of a tanning bed. Eyeing Morris, Derek dropped into the chair and lay back.

Morris turned to face him. He had a clipboard in his hand and a metal apparatus, all lenses and wires, attached to his forehead. He gave Derek a faint smile. "Nice to see you again, Mr Wrombsford."

"Likewise."

Morris surveyed his notes. "So, we'll start with a quick check up then get those photos taken. For a life insurance policy, isn't it?"

Derek shrugged. "Have to ask the wife about that."

The circles under Morris's eyes seemed to darken and the skin on his face drew taut. He perched on his stool beside the chair and plucked a dental mirror off a tray. "Open your mouth, please."

Derek stared at the ceiling while Morris probed about with his mirror, stopping every so often to scratch at something with a sharp probe. At one point, he stopped completely, got down on his haunches and squinted into Derek's mouth. It looked like he might say something but then he just shrugged and sunk back. He wiped off his tools with a piece of tissue paper. "You've got the teeth of an eighteen-year-old."

"Thanks, Mum always made me brush my teeth."

Morris shuffled through a drawer and produced a square device with an electrical lead hanging off it. "Let's get these pictures done and you can be on your way." He leaned over Derek and put all the pieces in place, laying the device on the tray.

Sweat ran down Derek's cheeks in rivulets. His mouth felt

awkward. He wanted to swallow, but didn't dare, fearing he might take in a wire. If someone wanted him dead, this would be their perfect opportunity.

Clutching a switch that looked an awful lot like a detonator, Morris trudged from the room. The lights went out. There was a flash. Morris re-entered and the lights came back on. "All done, Mr Wrombsford." He set about plucking all the pieces out of Derek's mouth.

Derek shifted to the edge of the seat and stood, holding out his hand for Moris to shake. "Guess I'll be seeing you then."

Morris nodded without turning around, the attempted hand-shake unseen. Paper slapped in and out of folders. Drawers slid open and shut.

Where were the man's manners? Who cared. Let the bugger have his backward ways. Derek slammed the door behind him, hoping it made Morris leap out of his skin.

He headed back downstairs thinking about heading to *Wanda's*. He hadn't been in ages. The thought of supple, teenage hands on his skin sent shivers up his spine. He crossed the reception without a word to the secretary. If she wanted to act stuck up, leave her to it.

A fresh breeze made Derek's nostril hair tingle. He crossed the road, trying to stifle a sneeze. A car engine roared in his ears. His stomach sank and he looked to his side.

A pair of identical faces stared back at him from behind a windscreen. There was a moment of indescribable pain followed by a distant concussion.

Then darkness.

Everything numb.

2

ETECTIVE ELLIOT KERR pulled up at the crime scene at approximately one thirty. He clicked off his seatbelt and stepped from the car.

Midsummer heat beamed down on the tarmac, turning the air thick and heavy. It had a certain sweetness to it. Kerr loosened his tie and jiggled his legs to shake off an uncomfortable sweaty feeling about his groin.

A tent, surrounded by yellow police tape, stood erected in the middle of the road. Officers and forensic scientists zipped in and out, like clowns of a demented circus.

Feeling a migraine coming on, Kerr reached up and stroked his temple. He stepped up to the tape, nodded to the officer guarding the perimeter then ducked under. "What've we got here?"

"Hit and run," the officer said.

"Anyone get the plates?"

"Car was found abandoned six miles away. We're checking for owners."

Kerr nodded and strode toward the tent. He pulled back the flap. It was cool and shady inside. He took a moment to enjoy the sensation then let his eyes drop to the ground, to the body splayed out over the road.

Its torso and legs looked normal. The head, however, was not. Pieces of skull and purple tissue decorated the chipped road.

It looked like someone had gone at a watermelon with a sledge hammer.

His stomach did a flip. He struggled to keep his microwaved lunch down.

Behind him, the tent flap slapped back. "Doesn't get any better, does it?"

Kerr turned around.

Detective Quinn stood there. She ran her eyes over the remains and winced. "Ever seen anything like this?"

"Shotgun is what I'm thinking."

"Wrong there, detective. Just a car."

Another surge of bile. Kerr brought his fist to his mouth to hide his rippling throat. "Who was he?"

"Derek Wrombsford."

"Never heard of him."

"No reason you should've. Small time. Couple of driving offences. Ran escorts. Toed the line but never really worth bringing in."

"So why's he dead?"

She sidled up alongside, patted him on the shoulder then smiled. "That's where you come in, buddy boy." She yawned and headed out. "My youngest kept me up all night. Chickenpox. Fancy a coffee?"

"All right."

She left him alone with the body.

A hot draught entered through a gap in the corner of the tent. Sweat seemed to pulse from Kerr's armpits. Coffee on a day like this? It made him glad he didn't have kids. Never wanted to.

He slipped out from the tent and emerged into the sunlight, which made him squint.

The same officer approached. "Can we reopen the road, detective?"

"Sure."

The officer waved to a pair of men with a gurney between them. They wheeled it into the tent and Kerr headed for the café sitting on the corner.

Quinn emerged with two freshly capped coffees in her hands. She passed one to Kerr.

"Thanks," he said.

"Anything on your mind?"

"Nope, nothing that stands out."

Quinn blew through the oblong hole in the lid, sending up a torrent of steam. She smiled. "I mean in your personal life. Any special lady?"

Heat rushed to his cheeks. That perennial question. He stared down into the blackness of his coffee. "No."

"Oh, come on. I'm always telling you about my kids. Why can't you give me a glimpse into the exciting private life of Detective Elliot Kerr: the City's Most Eligible Bachelor."

"That's hardly accurate."

"What're you talking about? You've got a steady job, a flat. No skeletons in the closet, as far as I know."

Kerr gulped down some more coffee then stared into space.

"Well? Never thought about calling up Susan? She's always pleased to see you."

"I don't think so."

Quinn stared at him, her gaze seeming to burrow through his eye sockets and into his skull. After a couple of seconds, it was impossible not to look back. Something passed between them.

It was almost telepathic.

A secret Kerr had never told anyone.

Quinn's smile faded and she looked away. She downed her cup of coffee and dunked it in a nearby bin. "Let's get back to base. Something'll turn up sooner or later."

A hollowness opened up in Kerr's chest. Blood surged through his veins, making his brain pulse. Quinn had seen right through him. He knew he'd have to *come out* eventually, but he'd never imagined it happening like this. So what if he'd never thought about a woman in a sexy way.

Did that mean he was automatically a rainbow flagger?

Perhaps those brainfuls of private fantasies: men greased, muscled, ready for action, couldn't be ignored any longer.

I T WAS A LONG RIDE back to the station. Neither said anything. Kerr pulled up into his assigned space. When he reached out to unclip his seatbelt, Quinn snatched his wrist. "If you ever want to talk about it, I'm here, all right?"

He chewed his bottom lip and stared out ahead, fixing his stare on the brick wall. "Yeah, that's fine. Thanks."

Quinn released his wrist and stepped out.

Kerr followed her into the station, along the corridor to the reception.

The receptionist, Susan, beamed at them both as they entered the foyer. She kneeled on her chair, passing a folder onto the counter, offering Kerr a glimpse of her ample cleavage, just about concealed by her low-cut top. "Witness statements," she said.

Usually Quinn gave him a nudge in the ribs as they passed by Susan's desk, but she did nothing of the sort today. She collected up the folder and flicked through it. "Thanks."

Susan's perfume wafted up Kerr's nostrils. Bitter and strong.

He tried to avoid Susan's fluttering eyelashes.

"Turn up anything at the scene?" Susan said.

Quinn shook her head. "Nah, nothing useful."

Kerr kept Susan in his peripheral vision, while concentrating on the long corridor which led to the offices. Susan squeezed her lips together, sank back into her seat then returned her attention to her computer monitor.

Quinn tapped Kerr on the arm. "Let's get cracking then."

Was there any polite way of shaking Susan off? Kerr risked a quick smile at her.

But she only had eyes for her computer monitor now.

Bright sunlight streamed in through the windows of Meeting

Room Two. Kerr yanked the blind cord and the room dimmed. Quinn laid the folder on the table and flipped it open. Two pieces of paper nestled inside. "Not much to go on," she said.

"Nope."

She slid one of the pages out. "Felicity Adams, Secretary." She swept the other statement alongside. "Hugo Morris, Dentist."

"Wrombsford had just got his teeth done?" Kerr said.

"He had a check-up then got some pictures taken."

"Pictures? What for?"

"Life insurance policy. Body identification."

Kerr furrowed his eyebrows. "Bit morbid."

"Yeah, you'd better tell that to his wife. She's the one who set up the appointment."

"Looks like that's our first stop then."

Quinn shifted her chair back, got to her feet and held open the door. "Ladies first."

"What's that supposed to mean?"

She winked. "Always wanted a gay best friend. Opens up a whole new realm."

Anger flashed through him, but he kept it under control. He worried whether someone had heard her. Without meeting her eye, he slipped past her into the corridor. "Just pleased to oblige."

4

ON THE WAY to the car park, they ran into an officer returning from the scene. Kerr approached him. "Anything turn up on those plates?"

"Stolen."

"Prints?"

"Nothing on the database."

Kerr trod on toward his car. "All right, keep up the good work. I'm sure we'll turn something up."

Quinn sidled up alongside him. "So, what do you make of him?"

"I'm a professional—I don't think about that stuff at work."

"Yeah, yeah. Whatever."

They got in, each shut their door and Kerr laid his palms on the wheel. "He's a bit on the young side, don't you think?"

Quinn grinned.

It took about forty-five minutes to get to Wrombsford's house: a white-washed cottage out in the country. Vines crawled up the walls and a four-by-four was parked at a diagonal angle in the gravel drive. Kerr pulled up on the kerb outside and gazed out from under the windscreen. "Decent taste for a gangster."

"Well, I trust your opinion," Quinn said.

Kerr clicked his door open and stood watching the property for a few moments. Whenever he approached bereaved family members, there was usually a support group hovering about. And the lack of one here either meant Mrs Wrombsford wasn't in or she wanted to be left alone.

Birds sung in bushes and a gentle breeze took the edge of the afternoon humidity. The path to the front door passed over a burbling stream. Kerr did up a button of his jacket. "Someone's put some work into this place."

"I'd like to get the gardener's number, that's for sure."

Kerr knocked.

There was a series of footsteps from inside, each followed by *crunches* and *creaks*. Old house sounds. The door squeaked open and a woman gazed at them. She was in her mid-fifties and dressed in a tight black blouse and jeans. Mrs Wrombsford. "Yes?" she said.

"Police," Quinn said. "Can we have a word?"

Mascara pooled at the corners of Mrs Wrombsford's eyes. Her skin was pale and stretched. Although she looked pallid, her cheeks weren't red. Not at all like someone who'd been crying.

Mrs Wrombsford stepped back. "Of course."

Quinn waved her arm at Kerr with the glimmer of a smile. He rolled his eyes and walked inside, following Mrs Wrombsford.

The interior was decked out with white walls, interspersed with thick wooden beams. Cracks splintered their varnish, like they'd been salvaged from shipwrecks. A thick, blond carpet unfurled under his feet. The place was warm and familiar. Homey.

"This way, please," Mrs Wrombsford said.

They arrived in a kitchen.

Mrs Wrombsford pulled back a pair of chairs at the table. "Tea or coffee?"

Kerr took his seat, while Quinn remained standing. "I'll look after that, Mrs Wrombsford," Quinn said. "Sit with Detective Kerr."

Mrs Wrombsford's dry lips gave way to a smile and she sat. "Thank you. Everything you need's in the cupboard above the kettle."

A large tank, filled with tropical fish, sat snug in the corner behind Mrs Wrombsford. Its motor whirred away. Kerr cleared his throat and withdrew a notepad from the inner pocket of his jacket. "Just a few questions, if you don't mind. I'm sure you're feeling quite drained following this morning's events."

"Yes." Her voice was faint, almost otherworldly.

Quinn clicked the kettle on. It spluttered and groaned. She scrabbled through the cupboards, pausing a moment to frown, then produced a transparent jar of coffee, which she went about measuring into a cafetiere.

Kerr found a fresh page in his notebook. "Your husband took out a life insurance policy recently, correct?"

"Yes, officer."

"Detective."

"Sorry."

"I understand you made the dental appointment for Mr Wrombsford this morning?"

"Yes."

"To get photographs for his dental records?"

"That's right."

Kerr caught Quinn's eyes moving between the two of them, like she was watching a tennis match. The kettle clicked off and the water bubbled down. She set about pouring the hot water into the cafetiere.

"When did you last speak to Mr Wrombsford?" Kerr asked.

"Just before he left. I . . . I"—her cheeks flushed and a single tear dropped onto the table—"*kissed* him on the cheek."

Quinn tiptoed over and gave each of them a cup of coffee. She retreated to lean up against the kitchen counter. Her phone buzzed. She checked it then returned it to her trouser pocket.

Kerr tapped his pen on the table. It gave a full, wooden sound. People could say what they wanted about Wrombsford, but he certainly knew how to spend money. "Is there anyone who might have had reason to harm Mr Wrombsford?"

"No. Why would they?"

He wasn't going to press her for the details of Wrombsford's job. It all had a habit of coming out in the end, anyway, and there was no way he was going to be the *shot* messenger. He flipped his notepad over, tucked it into his inside pocket and glanced at Quinn.

"All right, Mrs Wrombsford," Quinn said. "You've been extremely helpful in our investigation. We'll let you know if we turn up anything."

Mrs Wrombsford rose. "Thank you."

Kerr ushered her back down. "No need to worry, we'll see ourselves out."

"You wouldn't like us to call anyone, would you?" Quinn said.

"No, I want to be alone."

Quinn flashed her eyes at Kerr. "As you wish." She dragged Kerr out of the kitchen and out of the house.

"What do you reckon to her then?" Kerr said.

Quinn shrugged. "Who cares. I just got a message. They found explosives among Wrombsford's remains. They've taken the dentist into custody."

5

THEY SHOT BACK to the station. Kerr paced through the reception area, blanking Susan. A stench of body odour mixed with rusty steel—blood—hung in the air.

Perhaps someone had just brought a tramp in.

Kerr nodded to the officer guarding the lockups. The magnetic-locking mechanism buzzed open. Quinn hung about Kerr's heels, like a faithful terrier. Most of the cells were empty. Kerr marched on to the end of the row where they'd put Doctor Morris. He paused to look through the wired glass before pulling back the bolt and slipping inside.

Morris sat at a steel table with his hands clenched. He wore a white shirt with two open buttons and his sleeves rolled up, revealing a gold watch. Kerr took up the chair opposite, while Quinn brought the heavy door shut with a metallic *thunk*. "Got something to tell us?" Kerr said.

"What am I doing here?" Morris replied. "I don't know anything."

Kerr whipped out his notepad and slapped it on the table. He slid the pen out from its rings and rested it against his bottom lip. "Just some questions. Answer them honestly, for your own good."

Morris's hands shook and his eyes darted about.

"Wrombsford came in to take some pictures, correct?"

"Yes."

"And you took those pictures."

"Of course."

Kerr glanced back at Quinn. Her features remained neutral, her skin had taken on a tone of grey. She nodded. Kerr squared his shoulders. "And when did you put the explosives in his mouth?"

"What? What are you talking about?"

"Forensics found traces of explosives among Wrombsford's remains. You put them there, didn't you?"

Morris winced then his eyes fluttered closed. His entire body quivered and he fell over onto his side. A strange gargling came from his mouth then vomit puddled on the cell floor.

Kerr's stomach knotted. Both Quinn and Kerr stared at Morris for a few seconds before Kerr leaped into action. He rolled Morris into the recovery position and crouched by his side.

Quinn slipped out of the cell and a few moments later Morris opened his eyes.

Kerr helped him into a sitting position. "Are you all right?"

Morris stared into space. A thin film seemed to have set over his eyeballs. He retched but nothing came out.

Quinn returned with a glass of water and a towel, which she handed over to Morris. He accepted them. "Do you need a moment?" Quinn said.

Morris wiped his face with the towel then dabbed at the corners of his mouth. "No, I'm fine."

Between them, Kerr and Quinn got Morris back on his chair. Kerr rolled his shoulders and tried to lighten his tone. "We're just putting a picture together."

Morris's cheeks seemed to pale. It looked like he might faint again. He took a sip of water and puffed out his cheeks. "I have no idea. Sorry. I'm just a dentist I don't know anything about this."

Kerr didn't buy it. It was a good act, he admitted that much, but it wasn't going to save Morris. Everything pointed to him. Kerr drummed his fingers on the table. "What about the drivers? Can you tell me about them?"

"What drivers?"

"The ones who ran over Wrombsford."

Morris swallowed and shook his head.

Quinn laid a hand on Kerr's arm and leaned into his ear. "Let's leave him to stew for a while. We're not getting anywhere."

"Okay, Mr Morris," Kerr said. "We'll be back later if you've got anything to tell us."

Morris's whole face thinned. "You mean you're not letting me go?"

Kerr got up from the chair, held open the door for Quinn to walk out then said, "Not likely. You're our number one suspect."

Kerr stepped out into the corridor and slammed the door behind him.

6

"**Y**OU RECKON we've got something?" Quinn said.

Kerr glanced in through the tiny lockup window. Morris rocked back and forth on his steel chair. "It's too early to tell," Kerr said. "If he's involved he's not the main party." He produced a handkerchief, bent down and wiped a smidge of vomit from his shoe. "He doesn't have the stomach for it."

At the end of the lockup corridor, the officer stood. "Message for you, Detective Kerr."

"What is it?"

"Lady here to see you."

"Who?"

"Don't know—she's waiting in reception."

Kerr exchanged glances with Quinn and they strolled on to the reception area, where a young woman sat. She had pale skin and clutched her miniskirt between her knees. Kerr approached with his hand outstretched. "Pleased to meet you, I'm Detective Kerr, and this is my partner Detective Quinn."

She flinched then, recognising Kerr's hand, reached out and accepted it. "I've got information for you. About Derek Wrombsford."

They headed into Meeting Room Two. Through the gaps in the blinds, school children filed past on their way home from school. Bursts of laughter punctuated the frosty silence.

Felicity—the girl who'd just come in, the dentist's secretary—sat on the edge of her seat, as if preparing to run.

Kerr clenched his bottom lip between his teeth, released, then said, "Whenever you're ready."

She took a couple of deep breaths then looked them both in the eye. "Morris didn't have anything to do with this—he's innocent."

Quinn coughed.

Kerr said, "And why do you say that?"

Felicity tugged at her skirt, pulling a crease straight. "Can you protect me?"

"That depends," Quinn said.

"On what?"

"What you're about to tell us."

Felicity squirmed in her seat and she looked to her side, out through the blinds. "I need you to protect me from Derek Wrombsford."

"Wrombsford's dead," Kerr said.

She shook her head. "I mean his *people*."

Kerr chewed the end of his pen. "That can be arranged."

No motion then, as if someone had given her an electric shock, Felicity sat up and gripped the desk. "There are three killers."

"Names?" Kerr said.

"Thomas and Toby Gulls."

"Brothers?"

"Twins."

Kerr scribbled them down then looked up from his pad. "And the other one?"

"Hilary Wrombsford."

Quinn nudged Kerr. "Wrombsford's wife."

Kerr made a note. "Take us through the story from the start."

Felicity opened her mouth then closed it. She looked to her side once again. "I want assurances."

"Afterwards," Quinn said.

Kerr said, "Go on."

"Toby and Thomas wanted in on Wrombsford's business," Felicity said. "Toby's been having an affair with Hilary Wrombsford and she wanted Derek dead so they could ride off into the sunset."

"How romantic," Quinn said.

"Thought they'd kill two birds with one stone. Get the business for Toby and Thomas, while leaving Toby and Hilary clear for a fresh start."

Kerr said, "And where do you and the dentist fit into all of this?"

Felicity squeezed her eyes and a tear rolled down her cheek. "Thomas is my boyfriend—they got me a job at the dentist's. I had to let them know when Derek was leaving so they could run him over. The dental pictures were the only outstanding evidence for his life insurance policy."

"So," Quinn said, "a nice crisp pay-out for Toby and Hilary?"

"Yes, I suppose." Felicity sank back and her head dropped to her chest. "They hoped Wrombsford wouldn't recognise me, but I think he did. Maybe I was the last thought in his head."

"Addresses?" Kerr said.

She gave them to him.

Kerr jabbed his notepad, smearing a full-stop, then ripped off the page and handed it to Quinn, who got up, crossed the room and disappeared into the corridor.

"Am I in trouble?" Felicity said.

"Remains to be seen."

She produced a tissue and dabbed her eyes, to stop her makeup running. "But I've helped out Mr Morris. He can go?"

He shook his head. "We found explosives among Wrombsford's remains. We still have no idea how they got there."

"But what does that have to do with Mr Morris?"

"They were in his mouth."

She looked down at her hands and shook her head.

Kerr sighed then stood. He opened up the door. "You can go."

She nodded and filed past him, out into the corridor.

7

THE NEXT COUPLE OF HOURS passed by in a blur. Each suspect was brought through the reception. First in was Toby Gulls. He burst in, leaping about, trying to free himself from the hold of the two officers. His wild eyes settled on Kerr as he passed by. "What is this bullshit!"

The officers dragged him down into the holding cells without explanation.

The second twin entered about half an hour later, much calmer. Thomas Gulls, Felicity Adams's boyfriend. He walked with his head bowed, eyes fixed on the pale-blue floor.

The very image of the Condemned Man.

Hilary Wrombsford was last in. She kept her head held high and turned to Kerr. "You'll be hearing from my lawyer—I'll be out in the hour."

It looked likely. That was the only piece that didn't fit. He hadn't had any choice but to bring her in, though. Not since Felicity mentioned her name. He stood staring at the holding cell, trying to work out what to do when Quinn appeared at his side. "Why the long face?" she said.

"Can't think how we're going to get Wrombsford's wife."

She tapped her temple. "That's where you're wrong."

"What do you mean?"

"Found the explosives. Above the kettle in Wrombsford's kitchen. It was a strange packet, caught my eye earlier, but I didn't think anything more of it. New stuff. Sensitive. Easy to hide. Can be scattered about—concealed easily. Guess she must've laid them in his cereal—made it so they stuck between his teeth, the impact when the car hit him set them off."

Kerr grinned. "So that's all sewn up then?"

"Yup, I'll give them the word to release Morris and we'll go get a coffee."

8

THEY WENT to the café around the corner, taking up a table at the window. Quinn brought the order over and they watched the traffic pass them by on the other side of the glass. There were several minutes of silence then Quinn said, "Well?"

"Well, what?"

She jerked her head to the side.

Kerr looked.

A man worked away at a laptop. He was dressed in a dark-purple suit. Every ten seconds or so, he'd stop to sip from his coffee cup.

"He's been looking at you."

Kerr's stomach squirmed and he felt himself blush. "Really?"

"Go on," Quinn said.

Kerr swallowed his mouthful of coffee and leaned across the aisle. "Excuse me?"

The man blinked a couple of times then smiled. "Yes?"

"You look familiar."

"Really?"

"Yes."

The man scrunched up his eyes. "Yes, I've seen you in court, haven't I? Are you a policeman?"

"That's right."

"I'm a lawyer."

The penny dropped. Kerr remembered giving testimony. This man had defended the accused. "Is it . . . Ferguson?"

The man grinned. "Glad to see that I was memorable."

Kerr looked to his side. Quinn had disappeared. He was just in time to see her trudge past the window, waving. Words melted on his tongue. He stared into the man's pale-blue eyes. "Would you care to join me?"

The man snapped his laptop lid shut then picked up his coat and case. "I'd love to."

TURBULENT STRIDES
DANDY

1

SARAH PEERED in through the neck of the bottle. Peered down into the ginger liquid within, studied the way that the bubbles rose upwards, collecting against the glass, almost like cars jostling for position at the start of a race.

She breathed in the vapour.

Felt it sting her nostrils.

Get right into the back of her throat.

That stench of ginger and lemon peel.

She had seen her daddy grinding in those ingredients herself —with her own two eyes.

This was the stuff all right.

She didn't need any label to know for sure.

This was *Dandy*.

Up, above her head, she heard the *creak* of a floorboard.

Her blood froze in her veins and, almost subconsciously, she reached for the cork which she had discarded on the pantry shelf, and swiftly stuffed it back into the neck of the bottle.

She stared upwards, through the bright yellow light which gleamed out from the exposed bulb above her head. The bulb batted back and forth at the end of its flimsy wire, caught by the draught into the pantry.

Above her were the stairs. She could see their shovelled-out forms. And she could picture the darkness which swelled over them.

Or was it darkness?

Could there be somebody up there?

Waiting.

Hand on the banister.

Sarah gripped the bottle of Dandy tighter and then she slid the glass bottle back into its place, alongside all the other bottles on the shelf. She took a couple of steps backwards, reached up and tugged the light cord.

With a *click-clonk* the mechanism shut it off.

She continued to feel the warmth exuded by the bulb as she stood there, in the darkness, her hand now resting on the door-knob of the under-the-stairs pantry, listening out for any sound at all.

It was difficult to hear anything, what with the great amount of noise her own breathing seemed to make. And how her heart seemed almost like it was *thump-thumping* right in the centre of her eardrums.

She strained her ears.

Told herself that she *had* to hear.

That it was her *responsibility* to hear.

But, no matter how much she chided herself, she knew that she could hear no other sounds in the house. Most likely it had just been her imagination. Just something in her mind thinking to play tricks on her.

She looked back to the shelf.

To all that moonshine her father had cooked up.

All those bottles—unlabelled—of variously coloured liquids.

And every last one a truly noxious mixture.

If her father found her down here, in his pantry, there would be hell to pay.

No doubt about it.

More than that even . . .

She held still, only daring to breathe through her mouth. That seemed, to her, to make less noise than breathing through her nose. Or maybe it was just her allergies, that she seemed to have a perpetually blocked nose, constantly stuffed-up sinuses.

Her heart beat on.

Thick and concussive.

Almost seeming to strike her from within.

Like a traitor inside.

She held herself impossibly still and counted out the time.

One.

Two.

Three.

Four . . .

She waited till she'd reached a hundred before she dared turn the handle of the pantry, before she dared set foot back into the kitchen.

As she did, she was struck by the stillness, and by the way that the silvery moonlight tumbled on in through the uncurtained window at the kitchen sink. A stack of dirty plates stood precariously balanced. That stack of plates that she'd promised her daddy she'd get clean earlier tonight. But she hadn't got around to it. She'd had other things on her mind.

Like grabbing herself a bottle of Dandy.

As she stood there, alone in the kitchen, she felt her senses returning to her.

Like her courage was coming back.

It was funny, the way all the kids looked to her, like she was the bravest one they'd *ever* seen. She thought back to the time when their head teacher—Miss Frankly's—car had got buried in a snowdrift . . . and with Miss Frankly inside, at the wheel. And Sarah thought about how her heart had hammered her into action, and how she'd dug through that snow with her bare hands to free the car, and Miss Frankly.

Everybody had talked about how she'd saved Miss Frankly's life, said stuff about how Miss Frankly might've fainted, and died, from carbon-monoxide poisoning.

But Sarah didn't like to think of it in those terms.

She liked to think that somebody else would've stepped in, if only she'd held off for a moment longer.

In fact, she was sure of it.

And then there'd been the time, at the kiddies' pool, when she'd been with her friends.

They'd all been queuing for a turn on the high dive when she just happened to tilt her head—*just so*—and catch sight of the kid's head plopping down beneath the level of the water.

She could remember, quite clearly, how somebody—her best friend Mary?—had jabbed her in the back, had wanted her to keep up with the queue to the high dive.

And that had been what'd thrown her into action *that* time.

There was no end of anecdotes of stuff that she'd done . . . or stuff that they *claimed* she'd done.

But the truth was that she was just as scared about stuff as the rest of them.

And that this—this *swiping* her daddy's Dandy—well, this might rank as just about the most courageous act of them all.

She held still another few moments.

Looked back to the pantry door, still open.

Without thinking clearly, she slipped on in there, seized a hold of the glass bottle—felt its coolness, felt the *slop-slop* of the liquid inside—and then, just like the skittish little schoolgirl she really was, she skipped back up the stairs and hopped herself back into bed.

Only when she drew the blanket up to her chin, had the Dandy stashed in her school bag, did she allow herself a grim, satisfied smile.

2

THE NEXT DAY AT SCHOOL Flick Taylor—her best friend—bucked up to Sarah as she trudged along the hallway. Flick held her maths textbook clutched to her chest.

"You get it?" Flick said.

Just like always, Flick's eyelids were droopy-looking and she had on that dark-purple eye shadow which put Sarah in mind of a pair of black eyes.

Sarah nodded.

Flick gave her the sliver of a smile and then gave her a playful tap on her upper arm. "I knew you'd do it—*knew* it."

And, with that, Flick shunted on off up the staircase, in the direction of her maths classroom, while Sarah headed on her way to English.

Throughout class—her last of the day—Sarah couldn't bring her mind into focus. She concentrated too hard on the clock up above the whiteboard. Took in its metal frame which sheened in the sunlight which dribbled in through the slatted blinds of the classroom.

Those minimalist, thin, black hands *tick-ticking* their way about the white circular backdrop.

It was that stage of the school year where it was pretty much taken for granted that there wasn't much more that Sarah's teacher—Mr Greenwood—could do for them.

This was the last day of school before they'd all go off on study leave, to prepare for their exams.

As a result, Mr Greenwood was pretty lax about what they actually did in class. Though the theory was that they were all meant to be doing private-group study—something which made Sarah think of *oxymorons:* a term they'd learned for their exams—the reality of the thing was that they all just pretty much mulled about chatting about whatever while Mr Greenwood sat, fore-head resting on his upturned palm, marking papers for some other class.

The classroom was abuzz with chatter, and the smells of perfume as the girls got themselves geared up for the Big Exit. And the smell of deodorant as the boys did the same.

Everybody had their plans.

And Sarah had hers.

It must've been about ten minutes till the end of class when she heard somebody whisper her name from behind.

When she turned, she saw that it was Adam.

Though she didn't know him personally, they'd sat in enough classes together so that she knew him by name. He'd always struck Sarah as being a bit of a loser, that way he would skulk about school with that long, greasy black hair of his. Hands always stuffed into the front pouch of his black—it was *always* black—hoodie.

"It true what they say?" Adam said, flipping his fringe out of his eyes. "I mean, about that stuff your dad cooks up . . . the *Brandy?*"

"Dandy," Sarah corrected him. "It's called Dandy."

"Yuh," Adam said, his voice still a whisper. He glanced about himself to the rest of the room.

Sarah looked down at Adam's desk, to his exercise book he had open there, and she saw that he had a whole bunch of scrawled drawings within.

"Uh, so," Adam said, and then he glanced over Sarah's head, as if Mr Greenwood would be interested in what they were chattering about.

He wasn't.

Mr Greenwood remained fixed on the papers on his desk, pausing to make the odd scratch with his red pen here and there.

Adam looked back to Sarah. "Any chance of you getting me some of it—I mean, like, I could pay you or whatever?"

Sarah thought this over. She breathed in, and then out. Thought about the plan for this evening. How they were all meant to be meeting down at the creek a way away from school. She would meet Flick there, and five or six others.

Though they were all meant to be headed home as soon as possible to get studying for their exams, they'd all come to the conclusion that it'd be overall good for morale if they could have some 'balls-out'—that was the *boys'* phrase, not hers—drinking beforehand.

And that had been where Sarah's Dandy had come in—the reason why she'd been required to snaffle that bottle of moonshine off her daddy.

She looked to Adam, took in his pasty complexion, the way that his inky black hair looked like it had been submerged in a vat of cooking oil.

What did she have to lose?

So she told him about what they were doing after school, asked if he wanted to come along. She guessed that even loners deserved a chance to just let themselves go—get pissed—once in a while.

3

W ITH ADAM WALKING ALONGSIDE HER, Sarah's eyes flickered along the path before them. The elm trees which lined the pavement they walked down. The wind blew through them, making all the leaves rustle, and adding a pleasant late-summer smell of chlorophyll to the air. When Sarah lolled her tongue about her mouth, a nervous habit of hers which she performed whenever feeling a touch awkward, she tasted the sour note of her own spit.

As she padded along, she could feel the bottle of Dandy in her messenger bag nestled inside there, could feel it moving against her hip.

She glanced back over her shoulder, as if they might be being pursued, and when she turned her attention back to front and centre, she couldn't help catching Adam's eye.

Adam gave her a vague smile—one of those *stoner* smiles which carried a sort of happy-go-lucky gravity to it. "What you worried about?" he said. "It's like you think somebody's following us, or something."

Sarah managed the flicker of a smile. She broke off eye contact with Adam and concentrated on the pavement ahead. Concentrated on putting one foot in front of the other. "It's just that this—what we're doing—it's kind of a tradition."

"A 'tradition' how?" Adam asked.

She shrugged. "Dunno, I've just heard stories, about how this day, the last day before we all go off to study for the exams, how it's traditional for all the final-year kids to go out and get pissed down the creek."

They trudged along in silence for a few paces.

Sarah felt like she should fill in the lines a bit more.

From the looks of things, Adam was one of those that liked to ask questions so it was better for her to pre-empt them.

"The teachers know about it, of course," she said, "and there's always stories about how they've been over to check on students, to see if they're getting into any trouble. Thing is, the woods around the creek are so large that once we get there it won't be a problem. We won't get caught. But it's just the *getting there* that's the trouble."

Adam gave a sly smile, then said, "Sounds pretty lame that a teacher'd take time out of their evening to come and check up on a whole bunch of kids getting fucked up, huh?"

Sarah smiled back a little. "Yeah, I guess so."

They walked on another couple of moments in uncomfortable silence before Adam said, "And you don't think that I'm like a *spy* or anything, right?"

Sarah's chest tightened. She looked back at him. Saw that he was grinning from ear to ear, and she couldn't help grinning back. "Nah," she said, padding on, along the path, bringing the break in the bushes up ahead, and entrance to the woods, into view. "I think you're a pretty safe bet."

"Glad to hear it," Adam said.

But as they paced out those final few yards to the break in the bushes, Sarah couldn't help *just one more* glance back over her shoulder . . . just to be sure.

4

A FTER forty-five minutes' walking, Sarah brought the verdant valley into view, along with the long, out-of-control grass bursting up in tufts all over the place. She looked to the creek, the grey water which pattered along merrily over the granite rocks in the stream.

The sun beamed down on her cheeks as she emerged from the bushes and headed off along the path they'd taken to arrive here. She felt the warmth from the sunlight heating up her blood, filling her stomach with butterflies. As she wandered on, she breathed in the fierce smell of fruit—of *rotting* fruit—and she saw, up ahead, an apple tree with what must've been more than a hundred apples all lying about its circumference.

"This the place, then?" Adam said.

Sarah glanced to him. "Looks like it, doesn't it?"

Though Sarah had heard stories of the creek before, along with how she was to get here, this was the first time she'd actually stood in this place herself.

Actually looked over it.

Everything was like how they said, that on a sunny, summer's afternoon, like today, it really was something approaching paradise.

Kind of miles away from all the suburban sprawl they'd all grown up with.

And, as she thought of it now, an appropriate place for them all to say a kind of *farewell* . . . and for them all to get just a little tipsy along the way.

With one of her daddy's finest brews.

She felt a touch of ice enter her bones. Just to think about her daddy, what he might do if he found out that she'd snatched one of his bottles. But it was too late now, there was nothing that she could do short of head on home and replace it back where she'd found it.

That would be backing out, though, that wouldn't be coura-geous at all.

And she knew, right then and there, that she simply wouldn't be able to explain such a gesture to her friends in a way that they'd understand.

They didn't know her daddy like she did, after all.

Sarah and Adam took up a place in some thick grass a little way along. All told, it was about two or three hundred paces away from the opening in the bushes, and it gave them a good view of the path leading there. That way, if a teacher *did* happen to come sniffing around, then all of them—all the kids gathered around the creek—would see them right away.

"So," Adam said, staring on down into the creek, "you think I could see it?"

Sarah hesitated a moment, felt her heartbeat hum in her throat. Then she dug into her bag, past all the books snuggled in there, and she slipped the glass bottle out. Held the bottle up to the sun so that she could better see the translucent, ginger liquid within.

She handed it to Adam.

"No drinking," she said. "Not yet."

Adam took the bottle from her, eyed it the same way that she had, and then he sniffed at the cork, still stuck in the top there. When he looked to her, he was wearing a wicked smile. "You've already had a nip yourself, haven't you?"

"What do you mean?"

"You already popped the cork."

Sarah thought back to last night, when she'd had to sniff at it to make sure she'd got the right batch of Dandy. But she didn't have the energy to explain all that so, with a shrug, she said, "All right, if you really wanna . . ."

With a gleam in his eye, Adam popped the cork on out. He stuck his nose right into the glass neck, and breathed in heavily. He clenched his eyes shut, gave a splutter and then said, "Wow, that really is some stuff!"

"Yeah," Sarah said, looking vaguely back at the bottle, and then back to the break in the bushes where they'd entered the creak.

She checked her watch.

Knew that the others should've arrived by now.

But they weren't there.

She dug about in her bag, checking for her mobile.

She found it soon, looked at the screen, saw that there was a new message.

A message from Flick:

Plan's off. Somebody blew the whistle.

Sarah felt her heart tapping against her ribs. Suddenly she felt a strong warmth rising in her cheeks. She looked back at Adam, saw that he was swigging the Dandy down. His cheeks bulged as he swallowed it, a gulp at a time.

Getting to her feet, Sarah said, "Come on, we've gotta go."

Adam continued to swig the Dandy down till, she saw, he'd swallowed what must've been a quarter of a pint . . . if not a little more.

When he brought it away from his lips, he let out a strong sigh. He batted his eyelids a few times, and then thrust the bottle in her general direction.

Sarah crouched down and ran her hand through the long grass, searching for the popped cork. Soon enough, she found it, and she replaced it in the bottle. As she examined the remaining contents, she couldn't help saying, though she felt like she was channelling her mother to do so, "You've taken down a lot there."

When Adam didn't reply, she looked down, to where Adam lay, sprawled out on the grassy bank of the creek. He was staring up at the sky, his lips slightly parted.

She nudged him with the toe of her trainers. "Come on," she said. "We've got to go."

This seemed to snap Adam out of it. He blinked a couple of times, opened and then closed his lips before getting to his feet, stumbling about as he did so.

Sarah grabbed hold of his hoodie right before he almost took a tumble down, into the creek. She didn't want to think about how, if he'd kept on tumbling, he surely would've landed down there, in the creek, cracking his head open on that hard rock beneath.

It was a trek to get back to civilisation.

Together, they wandered onwards, along the bank of the creek, with Sarah helping Adam along as he—increasingly— swerved from side to side.

When they reached the bushes, the place they'd emerged from, he started to speak in slurring tones too.

"Youurrr good *purr*-son," he said, his arm draped about her shoulders.

Sarah tried her best not to breathe when he exhaled, and she guessed that, if she'd had a match, she could quite easily have started a forest fire, there and then.

They lumbered onwards, somehow keeping to the path through the forest.

Sarah could feel a faint chill in the air now, and she knew that night would fall soon. As they headed onwards, she found that the path beneath their feet appeared to disintegrate. She backed up a couple of times, not sure of where they were headed, but, in the end, was fairly convinced that they were going in the right direction.

Two hours later, Sarah wasn't so sure.

5

NIGHT NOW was rolling in, thick and fast, and it was difficult for Sarah to make out her own hand in front of her face, let alone any sort of path that they were supposed to be following.

As they'd gone on, she'd found herself having to support Adam more and more.

And now she was having a task of keeping him upright at all.

Right as they took another couple of steps, Sarah felt her knees buckle and, just like that, they ended up in a heap to the side of the path with Adam landing on top of her.

She felt fallen pine needles jab in through her clothing, into her skin.

She felt a hot flush of frustration wheel through her, and, on impulse, she gave Adam a shove. Felt that he was heavier than she'd expected and had to give it a second go. This time, though, she succeeded in getting him off her.

Adam rolled onto his side and she listened to him be violently sick for what seemed like an eternity. Then—thank *God*—he was still.

As she sat there, on the forest floor, she couldn't help thinking about how her muscles all hurt, about how her feet were sore, and how the air was now distinctly chilly.

They were in the middle of nowhere.

And they were *lost*.

Capital-'L' *Lost*.

She stared up, through the trees, to the night-time sky.

And then, because it had worked out *so* well the last three hundred times she'd checked, she looked at her mobile screen, wondering if she might have some signal *now*.

Nope.

What a surprise.

That message, the one she'd got from Flick, when they'd arrived at the creek, she'd received that while she'd still been in school, still in English class. If only she'd thought to check back then, before she'd wandered off into the forest with Adam.

She might've avoided this whole thing.

She felt her shoulders rise and then fall with a profound sigh.

Then she looked to her side.

To Adam.

He was lying on his back now. Eyes shut.

That was the worst of it.

How she was stuck out here—*in the middle of nowhere*—with a *drunk*.

Someone just like her daddy.

She continued to stare at Adam for a few more seconds before she had a prickling sensation down deep in her gut. Before she'd really processed what it was that had brought the feeling on, she found herself reaching out, touching Adam on the arm.

He was cold.

Really cold.

A few minutes back, in one of those drunk-turned-toddler rages, Adam had insisted on throwing off his hoodie, on tossing it off somewhere into the foliage.

Sarah had thought, momentarily, about going to fetch it, but she'd found herself so struck at being in this situation with a *drunk* that she'd made a point of just striding onwards.

But Adam only had a short-sleeved t-shirt on underneath.

And his flesh was *ice* cold.

Again, on gut-instinct, she reached over and felt his wrist for a pulse.

It was faint.

Nothing more than a gentle stirring.

Her heart wrenched in her chest. "Adam?" she said, already

feeling the panic creeping up on her, that odd tingling sensation passing through her blood. "Adam?" she said again, this time squeezing his wrist, digging her fingernails in.

Nothing.

She tried to encounter his pulse again, another couple of times, but this time she found nothing at all. Not so much as a faint *murmur*.

She glanced about herself, as if there might be some help forthcoming.

But what did she expect?

They were out here, in the middle of the forest, *alone*.

Her mind spun. She tried to get a grip on herself. Tried to calm herself down.

But what was she meant to do now . . . now that he wasn't *breathing?!*

Thinking quickly, somehow channelling into some deeply engrained training, she lurched forwards, onto her hands and knees. She looked down at his parted lips, the way that his throat seemed to open up like a bottomless pit.

She intertwined her fingers and set them down on his chest.

Pushed.

Once.

Twice.

Three times.

Was this even what she was meant to be doing?

Or was it just something that she'd picked up from films?

Only as she was preparing for the fourth compression, did she turn her attention back to those parted lips of his.

She *knew* what she had to do.

That she had to breathe air into his lungs.

She composed herself. Tried to keep her heart from beating out of control. And then she leaned over him. Breathed into his lungs. Tasted that sickly stench coming back at her, along with that sour taste of alcohol from the Dandy that Adam had swigged down.

He had taken too much . . . she knew that now.

Though the stench of vomit was almost too much for her to bear, she forced herself to continue, to keep giving him mouth-to-mouth. She knew that Adam's life depended on it.

With every breath she breathed into his lungs, she couldn't help thinking to herself that this was her *real* chance to prove to everyone how brave she was.

This was bigger even than when she'd snagged her daddy's bottle of Dandy.

This was life or death.

. . . But she had no idea what she was supposed to do!

Sarah kept on going, kept on compressing his chest, breathing into his mouth, until it became too much. Until she simply couldn't go on any longer. Until she had to give things up completely.

She fell back from Adam, feeling giddy, her head like it was a wiffle ball, not substantial enough to remain on her shoulders.

And she puked beside his body.

For a long time.

Till she retched up nothing but air.

6

SARAH GUESSED that she must've slipped away to sleep while she sat there, slumped at Adam's side. It was the moonlight that brought her round. How it shone down through the trees onto her sat there. She blinked a few times, then looked about her.

Looked at Adam's dead body.

He appeared to her like a reclining statue, the way his lips were parted, and his cheeks seemed almost sculpted, the way that they had a concave dip to them.

Her heart throbbed low and heavy, and she felt the chill clawing at her skin.

She was of two minds of what to do next.

There were two distinct options, after all.

She could continue to sit about here—*wait* for help—or she could be proactive, stride off into the darkness of the forest and hope that she might come across a road.

At the road she could surely flag down a car.

But that would involve leaving Adam here . . . leaving Adam's *body* here.

In the middle of the forest.

It would mean that she had failed.

That she *hadn't* been able to save him.

But Adam was gone . . . hadn't she already failed?

Shouldn't her focus be on saving herself now?

She sat about for another couple of seconds, shivering, her teeth chattering so loudly that she could barely make out her own thoughts.

For a second—and just that *one* second—she considered taking a nip of the Dandy.

That would add a lick of warmth to her bones.

Surely buck her onwards.

She only needed to look down at Adam, to see him lying so still—*deathly still*—to know that it would be an extremely bad idea.

Unless she wished to die also.

Out here.

In the forest.

Her mind bucked back and forth as she tried to decide.

And, in the end, she did the only thing that she *could* do.

She hoiked herself up off her backside and set off, into the forest.

Not looking back once.

S ARAH WALKED for the entire night.
        She listened for any sound.

But all she heard was the stirrings in the undergrowth, the *crack* of a twig here and there.

As she ventured onwards, the sky became lighter above her.

Day was breaking.

Saturday morning.

She thought about her friends, all of them, no doubt, in their beds, not thinking that anything was wrong—*they* would be none the wiser.

As she trudged on, her messenger bag, still stuffed full with her school books, made her shoulder ache, and she longed to toss it away, into a thicket here, or a bush there.

But she held on.

Knew that the bottle of Dandy was still snug inside.

And that she couldn't simply *toss* that away.

For one, it might look suspicious.

And, for another, she couldn't quite bring herself to rid herself of it.

Now that it had claimed Adam—that it had *killed* him—she felt like it carried an extra emotional weight . . . something almost sentimental.

Or maybe her mind was plagued by shock.

It wasn't normal, after all, not normal for her to have a . . . well, he hadn't been a friend but . . . an *acquaintance* die on her.

Sarah kept on her path till she could hear the gentle *trundle* of an engine.

A *car* engine.

She followed the sound.

Her heart beat faster.

She felt a cold sweat break out over her face.

She shuddered some more.

But she broke into a run now, concentrating hard on the direction of the sound, frightened that she might allow it to slip away and she wouldn't find it again.

She heard the engine thick in her ears now, though, and so there was no risk of that.

She kept on her way.

The fledgling daylight was now nothing compared to the bright, blearing white lights which shone between the trees.

Sarah held her hand up to her eyes to block the blaze.

And then she heard her name.

"Sarah? Sarah? Sarah?"

Her name floated on the morning breeze.

She felt almost as if her own name blew against her cheeks.

Cool and pure.

She went faster still, tripped more than a dozen times over roots sticking up out of the ground, lost her footing down countless rabbit holes, and then the vision came clear.

Her daddy's car.

Its engine trundling.

Headlights blazing.

Her heart skipped a beat when she saw his face.

And then, just like that, she was running—*running* hard.

She didn't stop till she felt her cheek butt against his hard, muscular chest.

His arms embraced her.

His fingers reached up and combed through her hair.

She had found him.

She had escaped.

For a couple of seconds, she lost herself in the sensation, in her daddy's heartbeat. Slowly other voices bled into her hearing.

She picked out their questions. All of them hurried, directed at her.

They wanted to know where Adam was—what had happened to him.

She drew breath, tried to stop herself shaking, and mostly failed.

But she got out the information.

All of it.

In one long stream.

One of the women there, a lady who looked to be in her mid-forties, with straggly, wispy blond hair, clawed at Sarah, but her daddy battered her away, seemingly effortlessly.

And, before she knew it, Sarah was sitting in the passenger seat, beside her daddy.

They were driving away.

Driving away from the forest.

8

O N THE RIDE BACK HOME, she told her daddy all about it.

And she cried, almost without pause.

Her daddy told her how Adam had been the one . . . the one who had tipped off the teachers, and then thought that it might be fun to tag along for the experience anyway, had thought that he could get away with being among them, getting his own kicks, while he was also giving them up to the teachers.

Back home things got weird for the next week.

Police.

In the house.

Asking her questions.

Notepads.

Audio recorders.

Video cameras.

She almost lost herself to all that technology—it was almost like a *stampede*.

And she was glad, finally, to get shot of them, and to have some time to herself, to think through what it all meant, what the experience she'd just passed through had *meant*.

It was only as she sat up at her desk, late one night, pen gripped tightly in her hand, the day before her English exam, that it struck her.

Maybe that was the connection that got her thinking about Adam—about how they'd both been in the same English class, and how he wouldn't be sitting the exam.

She wasn't brave at all.

She was just a scared little girl.

There was nothing more to it.

But should there have been?

As Sarah sat there, staring at the lined paper where she'd scrawled out, in blue ink, a practice answer to an essay, she wondered about what the others thought about her—what they *really* thought about her . . . and she kept coming back to the same answer, over and over again.

They hadn't been the ones brave enough to swipe her daddy's Dandy.

And they hadn't been strong enough to drink from it.

Or to live with its effects.

Not like she had.

AVENUE OF BROKEN GLASS

1

SIM STUDIED the video camera viewfinder and scanned the scene once more. Carnage. It was complete and utter carnage. Seventeen cars, the news reports had declared, all backed up, one into the other. Broken glass all over the place. No one had a clue what had caused the crash, but it looked certain to have been a chain reaction, someone had been distracted and, in that crazy second, had committed the oh-so fatal flaw.

He trod along the row of crumpled-up cars. Fire fighters still worked to free crushed occupants, while police officers took names and contact details from those freed, the ones unharmed by the accident. Blue and red lights flashed all around. Every few minutes ambulance doors would slam shut and the ambulance would drive off, while another would draw up—as if they were taking part in some morbid relay.

Thom sidled up alongside Sim and prodded him on the arm. "Come on, let's get out of here, eh? Go for a pint?" His eyes trembled in their sockets as he took in the scene before him. "All this, it's just a bit bleak. I'm already going to be having night-mares for weeks, why not just leave it there, all right?"

Annoyed by the interruption, Sim lowered the viewfinder from his eye. "Look, the whole condition of us sharing this project—you sharing my mark—was that we'd come out here together."

"Yeah, Sim, but it's not like you need me, right? I mean, you're doing all the filming."

"That's because if I handed the camera over to you you'd probably cause another accident, on the other carriageway."

Despite this side of the road having been closed off since noon, the other carriageway buzzed along like normal on the other side of the barrier. Sim noticed the necks craning in those passing cars, stretching to get a look at the accident as they went by—to see for themselves the traffic reports they'd surely heard on their car radios. And Sim was capturing all this, taking all this down to be picked through, examined, by future generations. The peculiar event of the 'car crash.'

Thom quietened down.

Sim continued to peruse the crash scene.

"Oi! You two!"

Sim sighed then peered over the top of his video camera.

A policeman strode toward them. His black hat, with its shining, silver star, bobbed gently from side to side as he approached. "What do you think you're doing here? Are you with the press?"

"The press?" Sim said, holding his camera down at his hip, pointing it at his toes. "No, we're not with *the press*."

"Then get out of here. You've got no authorisation. You're getting in the way of the clean-up."

Sim settled his tongue onto his lower lip. "We're not doing anyone harm, standing off to the side here, not hindering the ambulances, getting in the firemen's way. We're working on an art project, getting footage, see?"

This only served to further enrage the policeman. His cheeks coloured and he puffed out his cheeks. "An 'art project?' What in hell's name does *art* have to do with this? Haven't you thought about these people's families? Don't you think they'd have something to say about you making light of their situation?"

"Oh no," Sim said, "you're misunderstanding me, officer. I'm not 'making light' of their situation, in fact I'm doing quite the opposite. You see, I'm immortalising this scene, this moment of infinite refraction in these people's lives. They—"

The policeman held up his hand. "Cut the crap, would you? I'm not interested in hearing all this arty shit. I want you off my crime scene, end of. If you're not off it in the next sixty seconds

I'll have you arrested." He glanced down at the video camera in Sim's hand. "And switch that thing off right now, or I'll have it confiscated."

As the policeman walked away, Thom turned into Sim. "Well, you heard the man. Now let's go off and get pissed somewhere. Forget about all this."

However, Sim kept up his bold stare, watching that policeman's heels clip off back along the row of smashed up cars. He snapped the viewfinder into place. "Nah, I'm just getting started here. Haven't you heard of suffering for your art?"

Feeling the policeman's glare on his back, Sim led Thom out along the row of cars, away from the crime scene, as if they were being two obedient, if slightly disturbed, little boys. When they got out of the policeman's line of sight, Sim eyed the bushes at the side of the road. Keeping the camera held tight to his chest, he leapt down into the ditch and, bowing his head to avoid low-hanging branches, got onto the other side.

"Sim?" Thom said.

"What is it?"

"I don't feel comfortable about this. Just doesn't feel right."

"If you don't want to wake up with your knob cut off I'd come with."

Thom remained where he was, scratching his arm, looking up the road to the bus stop. "Haven't you got enough footage already? Enough to go on?"

"No," Sim said, crunching his fingers into fists, "I still haven't got to the heart of the matter. Then and only then can we ship off back." He rolled his eyes. "Come on, sooner we get the footage, sooner we can go."

"And you're sure this is going to get a good mark? Because if I go through all of this and you pull some sort of 'C' shit afterwards, get us stuck with that, then I'll be seriously pissed."

Sim snorted. "For you, my dear Thomas, a 'C' would be a

sparkling result. Don't forget that I've seen your sketchbooks."

Seemingly stumped by this comment, Thom hustled down the bank and leapt up the other side, joining Sim there. His complexion paled and his eyes widened. "Let's just be quick, okay? Don't particularly want to end up in a police cell for the night."

"Trust me," Sim said, "you'll be safe if you stick with me."

They crept along behind the trees, keeping as quiet as they could. Sim gripped the camera tight, waiting for the moment when he'd find a gap in the bushes and be able to look out. When they drew level with the pile up, he got down on one knee and filmed through the branches. Thom stooped down beside him.

Both of them kept totally quiet for the next few minutes as Sim swivelled his arm to take in the scene, going between the destroyed cars. When he reached one scene, a pair of fire fighters with the jaws of life, cutting away at the rutted passenger door of a purple hatchback, he absorbed the young woman trapped inside, beating her fists against the window, clearly in pain.

Sim zoomed in on her face. He inspected the wrinkles around her mouth, the panic in her eyes, her slightly parted lips. The trickle of blood at her temple. A tingle of excitement ran through him and he kept the camera fixed on her, totally absorbed in her struggle.

"Sim?" Thom whispered.

Sim remained absorbed by the scene taking place before them.

"Sim?"

"What?"

"Can we go now?"

Sim stared at the woman, her frightened eyes switching between the pair of fire fighters, her saviours. She would be safe soon and she would commence the process of forgetting all about this—what must be the worst day of her life.

He brought the arm of the viewfinder down and met Thom's eye with a sigh. "All right. We can go."

2

BACK HOME, Sim sat at his computer, clicking through the footage he'd got that day. When he got to that woman, beating her fists and struggling to escape, he felt his whole body stiffen. His muscles hardened up. He froze the frame on her face and noted her expression again, tried to empathise with her, put himself in her shoes. There she was staring right into the faces of her rescuers, seconds from safety. Wasn't that pure desperation? Pure will to live? Wasn't that what he'd sought to capture today, that, mostly vacant, struggle in the grey area between life and death?

He slumped back in his chair and traced her features. For his project he would put this all in monochrome. It would add an aspect of unreality to the whole composition, bring out that human intensity all the more without the distraction of colour. And to think that Thom had wanted him to pick up his camera and walk away from the scene. He would've missed that wondrous moment.

3

S IM was of half a mind not to allow Thom to put his name on the project, which he had since decided to name 'Avenue of Broken Glass.' Thom had been a destructor, a *saboteur*, if he'd had his way the whole centrepiece of the work would've been lost forever. But, feeling in a somewhat appeasing mood, he did allow Thom to be his collaborator.

They got their marks back a week or so later. Although Sim actively tried to keep himself detached from such silliness, the pure theatre that was the grade-giving process on his course, he couldn't help but admit to himself that he was excited.

In the auditorium, he took his seat in the middle of a row, near the back. He got there early, before any of the other students, and he noticed himself shaking. The anticipation of seeing that woman's face on the big screen, the sheer desperation just opened a hole in his heart, sent judders through his veins and blood rushing to his brain.

As always, they started about fifteen minutes late. Their teacher, James Filburn—who always demanded they call him 'James'—took his place at the lectern. Today he was better turned out that usual—his jumper only had three or four holes in the front. He placed both his hands on the lectern and read through a pre-prepared speech, general feedback and, hilariously, lessons he himself had learnt during the grading process. None-theless, a nervous spark crackled through the room. Before Sim knew it the big screen spurted to life in a burst of static.

The other films were predictable enough. The first featured a snake slithering its way through a garden, the camera remained fixed on its tripod for the whole five minutes, and Sim found himself restraining the urge to yawn long and hard. The next was little better, featuring a wannabe model—one of those girls on the fine arts course, no doubt—stretching out on a deckchair, sunning herself while rain—obviously induced by hosepipe—piddled down on her. Sim noticed James arching his eyebrows in pervy appreciation of this arty wet t-shirt contest. There was a sigh of relief among Sim's peers when the screen flickered to black. And that signalled the beginning of Sim's segment.

The screen flashed the title of the piece, 'Avenue of Broken Glass,' and then revealed the line of wrecked cars, crunched up, one upon the other, fire fighters dashing between them like frightened cockroaches. The camera panned as Sim walked along the rows, pausing every so often to examine a particular object—a shard of glass on the asphalt, a rogue screw and, in one case, a child's doll, part of its face caked in ash, its woollen hair fried.

Then there was the cut, as Sim recalled the policeman approaching them, telling them to get away, followed by the new image, the woman in the car. Every orifice of her face flared open. The inside of the glass fogged up where she hammered her fists and screamed out. She was calling out in silence. He had forgotten how long he had left the camera on her face. It must've been ten minutes or more. He felt another surge through him, the thrill of this volatile moment as she stared death right between the eyes. When the screen went blank and the image was gone, Sim was so absorbed by what he had witnessed that the applause only reached his ears several seconds after the fact. He looked about himself to the slightly scared expressions, a mixture of awe and appreciation, on their faces.

Thom gave him a playful jab in his upper arm, followed up with a sly grin.

James was standing, clapping his hands, a smile on his face too.

The briefest moment of satisfaction squirmed through Sim, and then it extinguished itself when he realised that that moment of desperation was lost to him, that he would need another hit, to experience that surge once again.

He suffered through the rest of the films, doing his best to keep his calm, not to flee the auditorium, concealing his wish to return home and watch that woman's struggle on a loop on his computer monitor. He found himself sweaty, growing uncomfortable in his seat. He squirmed.

When James finally let them go he felt like a caged animal set free by its keeper. He bounded down the steps, out of the auditorium and caught the first bus back to his house.

4

SIM FAILED to make it to class for the next few weeks. He fobbed off his teachers with excuses of a rare blood disease, declaring that he had to stay at home until he felt totally well. In truth he felt something like that, in that he just couldn't get that moment of desperation out of his head—it would drive him nuts if he didn't do anything else about it.

He kept one eye on the news, looking for another opportunity, another car crash he could go visit, video camera in hand, but nothing came up. He bided his time, sometimes watching those frames of the woman for hours on end. He would take his ruler to her face, examining the measurements, his protractor to investigate the angles, trying to study what made it so particular, how that image just got to him. And then he realised. It had been staring him in the face all along. *Desperation*. That was the name of his drug, that was what he needed.

He waited all afternoon, his whole body shaking, the palms of his hands clammy. He wanted this. It had to happen. He needed to recapture the moment. This would surely be the easiest way.

The door creaked open and Thom's familiar lunky footsteps sounded in the hall.

Sim braced himself, camera in one hand and Stanley knife in the other.

Ready to recapture.

Author's Note

Thank you for taking the time to read one of my books. If you would like to hear about my latest releases you can sign up for my newsletter here: www.aviain.com

Thanks for reading!

AV Iain

Eleven
A Short Story Collection

Copyright © AV Iain, 2015.
Published by DIB Books
All rights reserved.

Cover design and layout copyright © DIB Books, 2015.
Cover art copyright © Bruce Rolff / Shutterstock, 2015.